CULTURAL REVOLUTION

CULTURAL REVOLUTION

STORIES

NORMAN WONG

PERSEA BOOKS NEW YORK

FICTION
WONG
14780013
5 - 26 -94

Copyright © 1994 by Norman Wong

Persea Books, 60 Madison Avenue, New York, New York 10010

Library of Congress Cataloging-in-Publication Data
Wong, Norman, 1963-
      Cultural revolution : stories / Norman Wong.
          p.   cm.
      ISBN 0-89255-197-6
          1. Chinese American families—Hawaii—Fiction. 2. Domestic
fiction, American. 3. gay youth—Hawaii—Fiction. 4. Family-
-Hawaii—Fiction. I. Title.
PS3573.05815C85 1994
813'.54—dc20   9338827
                                                   CIP

ISBN: 0-89255-197-6

Designed by REM Studio, Inc.
Set in Centaur by ComCom, Allentown, Pennsylvania
Printed on recycled, acid-free paper and bound by Haddon Craftsmen,
Scranton, Pennsylvania

First Edition

ACKNOWLEDGMENTS

For your support and encouragement, I thank you: Jack Barth, Karen Bra-
ziller, Harlan Breindel, Peter Cameron, Ellen Currie, Stephen Dixon, Mark
Epstein, Chad Klinger, Elaine Markson, Patrick O'Connell, Leah Mason-
Oppenheimer, Susan Chung-Silverstein, Dean Uetake, and a special remem-
brance for the Harold Keables.

"The Chinese Barber" first appeared in *The Threepenny Review;*
"Stitches" in *The Little Magazine;* "Ordinary Chinese People" (in a
slightly different form and with a different title) and "Robbed"
in *The Asian/Pacific American Journal;* "A Nice Chinese Girl" in
Bakunin; "Chinese Movie" in the *Trestle Creek Review;* "Open
House" and "Cultural Revolution" in *The Kenyon Review;* "Cul-

tural Revolution" also appeared in *Men on Men 4: Best New Gay Fiction,* edited by the late George Stambolian.

I wish to thank the editors of these publications for their support.

N.W.

For

Faith Sui Ngan and

Cowan Woon Kau Wong

You young people, full of vigor and vitality, are in the bloom of life, like the sun at eight or nine in the morning. Our hope is placed on you. . . . The world belongs to you.

—MAO ZEDONG

I prayed to rediscover my childhood, and it has come back, and I feel that it is just as difficult as it used to be, and that growing older has served no purpose at all.

—RAINER MARIA RILKE

CONTENTS

CONTENTS

III

CULTURAL REVOLUTION

I

MAI WAH

MAI WAH stood protectively in front of the examination table where her grandson lay. The doctor's hand came from between the curtains and drew them open as he stepped into the partitioned section of the clinic. Mai Wah backed into the table when she saw how young he was. She hated all doctors who practiced foreign medicine. But there was another reason to hate this one; he did not look like the others — the older, feeble ones who had never dared to talk back to her. This one looked like a hoodlum. He was tall, his hair cut to the scalp like the Japanese soldiers who had invaded her village back in China. The young doctor marched over to her grandson, Wei. Mai Wah grasped the edge of the table. When the doctor pulled up Wei's shirt, she wanted to slap away his hands. He placed the flat, round

3

steel end of his necklace on the boy's bony chest, moving it all over. After a while the doctor stopped, stepped away, and spoke: "Your grandson has an irregular heartbeat. A murmur. His heart takes an extra breath after each beat. Beat . . . wish . . . beat . . . wish. Usually there is nothing to worry about. But in some rare cases this irregular heartbeat can cause problems in later life. Your grandson shows all the symptoms of a bad heart: poor weight, loss of breath, pale color, constant exhaustion." He paused to clear his throat. "Unfortunately, we don't have the facilities here in Macao to be able to examine him any further. I want to send him to a colleague of mine in Hong Kong. There a machine will take pictures of his heart and give us a clearer idea of what's going on."

Mai Wah shook her head in protest. Her wrinkled lips quivered. "No, no." She summoned up her voice. "I'm sixty-seven years old. I've never been to Hong Kong. There's nothing wrong with him, nothing that some home brew can't cure. I wouldn't have brought him here today if his father had not insisted." Her head continued to shake. The jade earrings, larger than the lobes they hung onto, danced. "I told my son there was nothing wrong with his son. My son was also sickly when he was little. He's fine now. He never saw a foreign doctor. Chinese medicine for Chinese people."

The doctor pressed on. "There will be no needles, no blood drawn, no pills. There's nothing to worry about. There's a chance there is nothing wrong with him. Wouldn't it be better to know this than to be constantly afraid for his health?"

Wei remained flat on the table. He listened to his grandmother's breathing. He looked upwards at the silver rods and hoops holding up the curtains that separated them from the others in the clinic. Voices cut through, loud and biting, reminding him of the dim sum shop where he and his grandmother had eaten breakfast earlier. There at the shop he had covered his ears to block out the noise. His grandmother hit his hands away and told him to settle down and eat, then she roughly wiped his ears with a napkin. The fatty pieces settled in his stomach and tired him immediately. After breakfast he could not keep up with her at the marketplace. When she stopped to pick at the spinach, which he hated to eat, Wei sat on a crate to rest. He kept an eye on her, afraid of losing her at any moment. When she moved over to the fish stand, he jumped up and ran to her side. Out of breath, he clung to her shirt. "You are just like your father," she would say. "Always sick." At home she would smear lily flower oil on his chest to cure his nausea. The sharp sweet vapors rose up into his nostrils. His head began to float and spin. The oil stung his skin.

"There's nothing more that we can do for him here," the doctor said. "You must take him to Hong Kong."

Hong Kong, Wei thought. His mother lived there. He missed her.

"I'll set up the appointment for you," the doctor continued. "The ferry leaves every hour on the hour. I go there myself twice a week. I am willing to travel with you and your grandson if his father can't take you."

Wei sat up from the table. He placed his hand to his heart. He wanted to jump off the table and run around the clinic.

"No, no! He's not going to any hospital in Hong Kong." His grandmother's sharp voice halted his thoughts and forced him back down on the table. The doctor wrote on a sheet of paper. "Call me when you decide," he said.

"Let's go, Wei," she said. When Wei sat up again he felt himself falling to the ground. "Don't wait too long," the doctor said. He reached over and hoisted Wei off the table. "For the boy's sake."

Mai Wah pulled at his hand, leading the way out through the curtains.

FROM THE terrace Wei watched his father walking down the cobblestone alleyway, his T-shirt stained blood-red with the sauce of the roast duck and pork he chopped all day at the Chinese restaurant down by the harbor. When his father disappeared into their apartment building, he wondered if he would remember the promise he had made to take him to the Portuguese restaurant on the mainland side of the city that evening for his birthday. His father had so excitedly described the Portuguese food to him: crabs with a spicy black bean sauce, so hot that it would make your lips tingle.

When her son, Lin, walked through the door, Mai Wah waved the bad report from the doctor in front of his face. "We can't go to the Portuguese restaurant tonight. Wei's sick." Lin walked past her into the bedroom and returned in a few minutes dressed in a clean shirt, the stained one in hand. Mai Wah took it to the kitchen and washed it in a waiting bucket of water. "We won't know what poison we will be eating at the Portuguese restaurant," she yelled. "The doctor told me that we should take Wei to a hospital in Hong Kong. Isn't that ridiculous? I've never been to a foreign doctor and neither have you." She stood at the kitchen doorway, holding the wet shirt. Lin rested his head back on the rattan sofa, his eyes closed. "Hong Kong!" she said. He was thin and frail like herself, like Wei. Nothing good had been passed down through the generations. "When you were sick, and oh, you were so sick when you were little, I gave you only herbs and teas."

She walked toward the terrace. There she stepped up on a stool and pinned up the shirt to the line. The setting sun illuminated the dull red stains. The stool wobbled as she stepped off it. "Lower the rope," Lin called to her. "You're going to kill yourself."

"If it's too low the sheets will drag," she said. "And besides, I can't lower it myself."

"I'll do it this weekend."

"Never mind." She was temporarily blinded by the transition from the sunny terrace to the darkened living room. "Why can't we just go to the Chinese restaurant down the street, like we always do?" She rubbed her eyes.

"I'm tired of Chinese food. I see it every day at that horrible restaurant."

"How can you be tired of Chinese food?" Nothing was easy for Mai Wah anymore, and it hadn't been since they had arrived in Macao—years ago, when Wei was just a baby. All she wanted was to spend her few remaining years in peace. They would be helpless after she was gone. Who would do the shopping, the laundry, boil the tea? She could let them go to the Portuguese restaurant without her. It would be like that in not so many years. The monk at the temple had told her to expect only ten more years. Fifteen if she were lucky. But how would they get along without her? She fretted over this question even in her sleep. She could stay home alone this evening, listen to the radio and prepare herself a small meal of rice and salted fish. That was all she needed. No foreign foods or medicines for her. She would be asleep on the sofa by the time they found their way home. If she didn't go with them, perhaps something would happen to them. They would lose their way. The sun set and the room blackened. They should leave soon if they were going at all, before it got any later.

"Wei is too sick to go."

"Then take him to Hong Kong."

AT THE Portuguese restaurant Lin and Wei crunched crab shells, their tongues searching for the juicy meat as the sauce slid down their chins.

"Eat your crab," Lin said to Mai Wah.

"I don't want it. I won't be sick tomorrow," she declared.

"For heaven's sake, if you're not going to eat, why did you bother to come in the first place?"

"And let you two fools get lost in the cab over here? You probably would've ended up back in China." The crabs smelled salty and pungent like the harbor. A hulking mass of hard orange shells and twisted claws, covered with a lumpy brown sauce. She held her breath. She would not be sick tomorrow, she thought again. Wei picked out another piece. No use wiping his hands now; they'd just get dirty again. She stared over at the other patrons of the restaurant with amazement. There were even a few white tourists, and a crowd had formed at the doorway. All the way to this side of the city just for this kind of food. Through the window the mountains on the other side of the border, jagged and hulking, made her remember the rice village where she was born and had lived so many years of her life. She shuddered at the thought that she would have to die in Macao. She feared for her spirit not being able to find its way back across the border.

One calm day out of the blue her son had told her that they were moving to Macao. The riots, reforms, and killings were all moving southward. It was time to get out. China had lost its mind. Mai Wah did not have enough time even to arrange for her furniture and things to be packed and shipped. Besides, it had already been too late. Everything had been given to a neighbor whom she despised. The day they left she had only enough time in the morning to make a trip to the temple and an offering to the monks, and though she begged humbly for good fortune with a little red envelope of money, they refused her. She left the temple, cursing them under her breath but then regretting this as she boarded the bus. She imagined a great disaster falling upon them as they crossed the border.

Lin and Wei devoured the crabs; broken shells littered the plastic tablecloth. Mai Wah's portion lay cold, the sauce congealing.

"You know, Mother," Lin began, "I should go with you to Hong Kong."

"No one's going to Hong Kong," she lashed back. Her eyes refused to meet his.

"I thought that we might stay overnight there, with your brother's son."

She looked back at him. "What are you talking about now?"

"Maybe we should think about moving to Hong Kong in the near future. I heard the restaurants there pay more. Lots of foreign trade coming in. Tourists all year round."

"When did you get this silly idea in your head?"

"I'm thinking about Wei's future," he continued. "There will be nothing for him in Macao when he grows up. We should take him to Hong Kong now so that he can get a head start on his life. Maybe get him into a good school there. It's not impossible. We're not in China anymore."

She could not imagine going to Hong Kong for a day, let alone to move there, to die there. . . . Her son avoided her stare. He could never look at her when she was angry. Just like Wei. It was as if they wanted her to be gone sooner than she would be. She laughed to herself, thinking how they would never get along without her. They would be in even more danger in Hong Kong. Mai Wah had rejoiced when Ching Ai, Wei's mother, had left for the big city. She had always considered her daughter-in-law an opportunist. Ching Ai was an orphan without a dowry who used her good looks to trap Mai Wah's weak son. Mai Wah assumed all along that it was she who had orchestrated the move to Macao. "Has Ching Ai written to you?"

Wei played with the shells. A claw fell off the side of the table.

"Stop, stop," Lin called out. He swatted his son's hand. "Clean him up, Mother."

She took a napkin and began to scrub at Wei's chin. He wanted to pull away but was held in place by his father's hand on the other side.

"Well, has she written to you?"

"Yes, but that has nothing to do with why we should think about moving to Hong Kong. Do you want to see your grandson working in a kitchen like me? That might not even be possible for him if he is always as sick as he is."

"I'm not going to Hong Kong." Her voice rose above the cackle of the restaurant. "I'm not going to Hong Kong to live with Ching Ai. You should've never married her in the first place."

"She has nothing to do with this. Why do you have to bring her up?"

"She has been nothing but trouble since you brought her into the family. We're not going. Wei will never survive the ferry ride. He'll be sick every day in Hong Kong."

Wei murmured. "I want to see Mommy."

Lin released his son's shoulder and collapsed back in his chair.

"Quiet." Mai Wah clutched the dirty napkin and turned her eyes toward the window again.

LATE THE following afternoon, when it had grown unbearably hot in the apartment, Mai Wah took Wei to the park, where they sat with the other grandmothers. Their grandchildren climbed onto a nearby banyan tree with its many tentaclelike aerial roots falling to the ground from its outstretched trunk. The tree's mammoth trunk was not one solid piece but rather many limbs in a twisted pattern, rising high to the sky. New roots rained down from the umbrella of dark green leaves, seeming to grasp the ground to grow into limbs themselves. The children climbed in between the limbs of the trunk, an earthly playhouse. Mai Wah sat on a park bench as Wei stood between her knees. At times she drew them in against his waist, locking him in place. On the other side of the tree, fortune tellers set up stools and card tables, and displayed identical drawings of a man's face carved by lines into sections, each section a different color and labeled with a group of characters. Each part of the face revealed a different aspect of personality. The forehead, for example, foretold virility. Mai Wah considered these fortune tellers phonies.

Wei looked up at the tree, imagining climbing to the top. He feebly attempted to free himself from his grandmother's hold, failed, and began instead to tilt back and forth as if he were on a carnival ride. The carnival had come to this park last spring. He and his father had mounted the big wheel. He had never seen a wheel so large before. The people on board screamed and laughed. The wheel rose to the sky. Wei could see the entire city: the buildings, the water, the boats, but all for only for a moment before being plunged faster to the ground. The wheel would not stop.

Now Wei slowed his movement and then stopped as his grandmother's knees released their hold, the revolving wheel's handle coming undone. He felt dizzy and stepped away from her toward the banyan tree, which resounded with children's screams. He ran to the tree and in a breath inserted himself between its limbs. The bark scratched his legs, his face and his arms, and a body flew over him, jumping from branch to branch. Wei crawled on the ground, his knees tripping over the exterior roots. He stopped at an opening between two limbs. Bringing his head down, he crawled in. Laughter echoed in the hollow womb. He needed to rest.

From the bench Mai Wah searched between the limbs of the tree for Wei. She wondered if he had fallen yet. She told herself that it was healthy for him to play with the other children. The other grandmothers engaged in idle gossip. She did not have time to listen to them. Her eyes followed their jade bracelets from shriveled arm to shriveled arm. She looked down at her own bracelet. She had not taken it off since she had forced it on more than fifty years ago. Over the years, the bracelet had achieved a unique blend of green and white. She had been told that the richness of its colors reflected her personality. For a moment it seemed to threaten to fall off. She shook it, but still it clung obediently to her wrist, an extension of her own flesh and bones. Her jade would fetch a small fortune after she was gone. She feared that Lin would squander the money.

"Oh, there's nothing wrong with him," Mai Wah interjected into the continuous chatter. "Nothing that some home brew cannot cure."

Another grandmother spoke up. "A Hong Kong doctor will just fill him up with pills. They'll give him shots and take his blood. That surely can't be good for him."

The air hung thick upon the branches, but this did not stop the children from playing. Mai Wah still could not see Wei. She wondered if he was stuck between the limbs, unable to free himself.

Her son's proposition to move to Hong Kong rang in her head. When she was little, a great drought had forced her family into the big city for a while. Her father had worked at the factory. Every day she and her mother would search the city for food. Beggars, women and children, sat crying at every street corner. Her hand was sore from clutching her mother's shirt sleeve. Her mother moved quickly among the crowd as if she were trying to lose her.

The afternoon threatened to come to an end. Her eyes frantically searched the banyan tree for Wei. The other grandmothers, one by one, began to take home their grandchildren, who had obediently returned to them.

Wei climbed out of the cave. He wondered if he would always feel this way. He pried himself free from the tree limbs. He saw his grandmother staring at him. Behind her the restaurant and shop lights and billboards lit up. He remembered the carnival again. He stepped in between her knees.

"Listen to me," she began. "I was working in the rice fields at your age. My mother was always sick, and I had to take care of my brothers and sisters. My father worked all day, every day. When the rain didn't come we weren't sure if we were going to live or die. I didn't have time to be sick."

Wei climbed up onto the vacant seat beside Mai Wah and lay his head down on the hard wood. He pulled his knees up as his stomach turned and then closed his eyes, shutting out the burning lights.

"What's the matter?" she asked.

He vomited by the side of the bench.

When Lin arrived home that evening, he complained about the diarrhea he had had all day. Mai Wah immediately blamed the Portuguese food. She also quickly pointed out that she wasn't sick because she didn't eat any of it. She busied herself preparing more medicinal tea, this time in a larger pot with enough water for twenty bowls. Bark and root boiled to the top. Lin joined his sleeping son in the bedroom.

She woke them and gave them their tea, followed by a simple dinner of rice, boiled spinach, and salted fish. After the meal, Wei returned to the bedroom while Lin read the paper and Mai Wah cleaned up. No further words were exchanged that evening, and soon her son also returned to the bedroom. She turned off the light and lay down on the sofa.

WEI AWOKE in the middle of the night, the bitterness of the tea in his mouth. His father snored on his side of the bed. From the next room he could hear his grandmother's restless movement on the sofa. His side of the bed was pushed up against the windowsill. When he woke habitually in the middle of the night, he looked out of the window. A stray dark figure passed in the alleyway below, footsteps clacking on the cobblestone. It was heading in the direction of the casinos and hotels by the harbor.

Wei's mother had been a chambermaid there. At night she came home and told him stories about the funny English tourists. She walked around the room, rigid, her head held high, her hand dangled near her side, imitating them. Every weekend his mother would insist that they spend the day walking about town, from the top of the hill down to the harbor where the rickety fishing boats and junks, homes to small families, crowded beside the mammoth floating casino-restaurant with its pale red sides discolored by the constant movement of the polluted water. In the afternoon they would stop at a noodle shop for lunch and then at a sweet shop for sugary bean soup, cold for the summer, hot for the winter. His mother was beautiful; she had long dark hair and white hands. Wei held her hand like a boyfriend on a date, while his father and grandmother trailed behind them. Wei hated looking back. His mother seemed immune to them. She would laugh and talk only to him and point out the funny English tourists.

Each morning before she went off to work, his mother would carefully apply her makeup, powders, and lipstick in front of the mirror on the wall beside the worship shrine with its Buddha statue and bowl of sand stabbed with the dead butts of incense sticks. She would light a single stick, always followed by his grandmother's protest. Mai Wah did not like the sweet smoke, which lingered in a white thread up to the ceiling where it hovered before a small breeze ushered it out the terrace door. As his mother perfumed herself, Mai Wah adorned the shrine with a bowl of rice and replaced the old dried concave orange with a fresh one. His mother ignored her and concentrated on her own face in the mirror.

Wei remembered vividly what had been the final weekend before his mother had gone off to Hong Kong. They had dared to go into the floating casino, crossing over the walkway connecting the dock to the glass doors. Inside, people stood in front of silver boxes, pulling down handles as they carefully watched the machines' spinning eyes. Wei turned his attention to one machine, from whose mouth coins dropped and clattered. He was amazed by the sight of all that money. His mother pulled him on into the center of the room, where the fluorescent light of the *li*-high ceiling fell brightly like sunlight on the crowds of people gathered around bed-sized tables. There were dock workers, their dirty shirts buttoned up to their necks. The English tourists wore shirts whiter than their own skin. They stood tall and rigid, and on top of their big heads sat straw hats rimmed with colorful ribbons. The Chinese businessmen were dressed in dark suits, with identical short haircuts. Unlit cigarettes dangled from their lips as they leaned forward over the table, setting down red and blue coins. The final group—a sprinkling of old Chinese women like his grandmother— clutched their colorful chips in their bony hands as they stared at the table.

His mother picked him up. Together they watched the frantic movement at one of the tables: a rainbow of chips fell across the grass-green cloth divided by lines and decorated by characters and numbers, like the fortune tellers' drawings. Two beautiful women in identical red dresses stood by themselves at one end of the table. Like his mother, they were made up with powders and lipsticks, their hair combed and pinned back in place. Wei imagined the smell of their sweetly perfumed skin. One woman picked up an ivory dome lid and placed it over a small round wooden plate containing the magic dice. She then picked up both dome and lid, clasped together between her hands. A diamond ring was fastened around one of her fingers. She shook it all up and down, toward and away from her face. A rattle sounded from within. The other woman waved her white hand at the table and screamed, "No more bets." The first woman set the dome back down. Slowly the sparkling ringed hand lifted off the lid. Screams and shouts rose in a single surge and rebounded among the casino patrons. The second woman gathered up coins and placed others down on growing piles. Hands reached out, picking up and putting down more coins simultaneously.

"Go ahead, Lin," Wei's mother began. "Place your bet."

"You'll surely lose your money." Wei heard his grandmother's voice. He looked for her in the crowd but could see only the thinning silver top of her head, shifting constantly amidst those of the other patrons. His father held up his coins as his eyes focused on the table. Wei leaned in closer to his mother. "Put it down." Her voice rang in his ear.

"No." His grandmother had been swallowed by the crowd.

His father's hand seemed unable to propel the coins buried in his palm.

"Last call," cried the woman with the bowl. Wei saw his father's hand fall to his side. "No more bets!" The bowl rattled furiously.

As they made their way out through the crowd, Wei, still in his mother's arms, looked back at his father and then at his grandmother even further behind, pressing herself through the crowd. His father called back to her.

"If she can't keep up, let her go," his mother said under her breath as they passed through the glass doors and stepped across the rocking wooden walkway. Wei looked back to watch his grandmother nervously crossing to shore.

His father snored and his grandmother murmured. He didn't feel as tired now as he would in the morning. He wanted to run down to the harbor. Then he realized that if he were sick enough his grandmother would have to take him to Hong Kong, where he would see his mother again. He thought of her visiting him at the clinic there. She would probably be able to spend only a little time at his bedside before having to return to work.

FOR THE following few days Wei was too ill to leave the apartment. At her son's insistence, Mai Wah called the doctor at the clinic to set up the appointment in Hong Kong. When the doctor asked if she needed his assistance and said that Thursday would be a good day for him, Mai Wah thought she heard a cocky tone in his voice. "No!" she answered. "My son will take us." She took down the directions to the hospital from Hong Kong harbor. She was sure that they would never be able to find their way.

The day before the appointment, Mai Wah asked an old woman neighbor to watch Wei while she made a solitary journey to the temple. She needed to discover the fortune for tomorrow's trip. Although the neighbor had long been abandoned by her own children, Mai Wah had no choice but to ask her. From the street she looked up at the terrace. Wei sat on the stool, looking down the alleyway. The neighbor stood over him, her face blocked by a white sheet blowing on the line.

Mai Wah braced herself against the wooden doorway of the temple, her other hand to her heart as she climbed over the threshold. Her eyes widened. Monks were preparing for a funeral at the other end of the courtyard. A paper house about three feet tall stood propped up on the ground. Windows and doors were cut out of its paper walls; stick trees decorated its miniature front yard. It was a funeral service for an important patron of the temple. Mai Wah could not expect this kind of elaborate service for herself.

She climbed the stairs into the center house of the temple. A smiling Buddha, gold and gigantic, towered over her. Immediately, the incense smoke intoxicated her. She hurried out a back doorway with her hand over her mouth but stopped herself just beyond the threshold; her fear of appearing irreverent made her return to the shrine. She picked up a fresh incense stick, lit it against a smoking red-tipped one, and stabbed it into the overcrowded cauldron, all the while holding her breath. She nodded once more before leaving the room again.

In the next room, three monks kneeling on cushions recited quiet, fervent prayers to idols lined up against the wall. Their heads bent forward and their hands grasped their bead necklaces as they rocked themselves back and forth. They could not be disturbed. It was in the next room where Mai Wah hoped to find someone to read her fortune. She reviewed her questions about her grandson's health, the safety of the ferry ride, her son's desire to move to Hong Kong. Was the move a foolish notion? And finally, if there was enough time, the question of her own life expectancy. She occasionally asked this question, hoping that the number of years would have increased.

But the next room was empty. She wondered if it was already too late—all the monks would have to take part in the service. Would she board the ferry tomorrow ignorant of her own fate?

A billowing orange robe appeared at the doorway. An ancient monk walked into the room. Mai Wah rushed to block his way.

"I must hurry," he said to her.

Mai Wah concentrated on his robe; her lips trembled. "I need a fortune."

"The funeral is about to begin. I don't have time right now."

She produced from the pocket of her blouse, near her heart, a tiny red envelope. She held it up to him. He retrieved it without a word and tucked it away into the cave of his sleeve. She steadied herself with her hand against the furniture, the shrine, the doorway as she hurried to keep up with him.

She followed him down several hallways, making a series of turns, all the while fearing that she would not be able to find her way out alone. The sound of the drum grew louder. They were moving toward the front of the temple. All she had to do was to listen to the drum's pounding to find her way out.

In a small room, the monk seated himself on a wooden stool. Incense smoke filtered through the air. Mai Wah held her hand to her mouth and sat down beside him. When he gave her an impatient look, she brought her hand to rest in her lap and breathed deeply. In her mind she tossed her questions about. Slowly she began, "My grandson Wei is ill. We must go to Hong Kong tomorrow to see a doctor there. Do you advise such a journey?"

The monk removed his hand from the interior of his sleeve and picked up the small red fortune book from a nearby table.

"If this journey is already scheduled for tomorrow, why do you come to me today?"

"The decision was beyond my control," Mai Wah muttered, but her answer went unacknowledged. Without looking up from the pages, he said: "Your grandson is in some kind of danger. Perhaps he is ill and must go to Hong Kong. Be careful tomorrow. That is all I can advise you now." The banging of the drum ceased. The monk rose without another word and passed through the clouds and out of the room.

Standing up, she felt faint and reseated herself. She hated feeling this way, too weak even to walk. She imagined Wei feeling this way on many occasions. How horrible for him, day in and day out! She told herself to put aside her stupid superstitions. Tomorrow they would take him to Hong Kong. She stood up and moved to the doorway, envisioning the way out. She heard the crackle of the fire and proceeded down the hallway, all the while bracing herself against the wall.

Outside in the front courtyard, red flames burned out of control. She could see the skeleton of the toy house. The monks encircled this second sun, their orange robes a bracelet around the fire. Curious visitors blocked the doorway and barred her escape from the temple.

SHE CONSIDERED herself fortunate to find an unoccupied bench in the waiting room. The ferry was not scheduled to arrive for another thirty minutes, but already all the benches had been claimed and a small crowd gathered near the closed doorway. Their proximity to the door worried and agitated Mai Wah. If more people were to stand there and be the first to board, then there might not be any seats left by the time she managed to pull

Lin and Wei aboard. What if they were forced to stand for the entire ride? But she soothed these anxious thoughts by deducing that when the ferry did arrive, its passengers would first have to disembark before anyone would be allowed on. Then the people gathered nearest the doorway would be asked to move aside or, better yet, would be pushed aside by the exiting crowd. Because of this, she would have just enough time to gather up Lin and Wei and hurry on. The people on the benches could not be pushed aside by the crowd. She congratulated herself.

Lin leaned his head back against the wall and closed his eyes. He was tired, he told her. This morning he had gotten up an hour earlier in order to work an extra hour, so that he could take the afternoon off. Wei sat on the edge of the bench, gazing at the growing crowd. She worried that the ferry ride would make him even more ill. He appeared surprisingly energetic. It was as if he were looking forward to this trip.

Fifteen minutes remained before the noontime ferry was scheduled to depart, and still there was no sign of it. More people continued to crowd in. Mai Wah listened to a circulating rumor that the ferry would be late; it had stalled somewhere between Hong Kong and here, in isolated waters. Another rumor began, something about a sinking ship, but this possible disaster was quickly ruled out by an announcement over the loudspeakers that the ferry would be late due to a small technical problem. Mai Wah remembered the monk's words. She felt for the pack of biscuits inside her purse, which she had brought in case Wei became hungry. If they were stalled on their journey in isolated waters, then the biscuits would prove invaluable. Heaven forbid a greater disaster.

Wei looked forward intently. Bodies rubbed up against each other. Perspiration ran down the backs of necks. Grand-

mothers fanned themselves, clipping the people around them. Voices rose. The familiar sick feeling returned. The thought of being like this for the rest of his life depressed him. A man bumped into their bench. His grandmother gave the man an exasperated look. Wei felt terrible for her, having to take care of a sickly child like himself. How much easier it would be for her if she were free of him. She shifted in her seat, avoiding the people around her. He closed his eyes in order to hide.

Time passed, and still there was no sign of the ferry. The crowd pushed even closer toward the doorway. The monk's words sounded in Mai Wah's head. She reached over to wake her grandson. "I hate crowds," she began, "Wei . . . listen to me." He opened his eyes, and she held him in her line of vision. "I have a story to tell you about something horrible that happened back in your father's village in China." Lin began to snore.

"Once there was a terribly outspoken boy in our home village. He always went against his mother's wishes. He would not get along with the other boys his own age and instead chose to hang around the field hands, listening to their fantastic stories of the city. He demanded that his mother take him there. She would sadly refuse him. She had the household and her daughters to care for. He threatened to run away. He spread rumors that she did not care enough for him. On his twelfth birthday she yielded to his pleas—the power of the only boy in the family.

"One weekend she left her daughters with a neighbor and boarded the bus to the city with her son. There he saw things he had never seen before: hundreds of bicycles racing by, peddlers selling every kind of ware and food, fancy restaurants in a row, stores filled with unusual trinkets, and more people than he had ever seen in his lifetime. While all this amazed him, it frightened the mother."

The sight of a group of half-breed teenage boys, Chinese and Portuguese, their eyes big and round, their skin dark and smooth, distracted Wei from his grandmother's story. White T-shirts and blue jeans clung to their muscular bodies. Their brown hair was greased back, cigarettes dangled from their lips. They forced themselves through the crowd, past Wei, to the front of the doorway.

"Listen to me." Mai Wah held onto his arm. "The mother clung onto her son's hand as they pushed through the crowd. When she felt herself being pulled along by the crowd, she tightened her grip."

Wei wanted to pull away from her so that he could get a better look at the teenage boys. The crowd complained about the delay and cursed the boys. The boys swore back at them and lit their cigarettes; white smoke rose to the ceiling. Ashes fell onto the sweaty T-shirts of other men.

"Somehow the mother became separated from her son. He instantly disappeared. She pushed herself through the crowd. Her motions were slow and futile, and she feared that she was taking herself even further away from him.

"It grew dark in the city. She stayed overnight and the next day returned to the site where she had lost him, retracing her steps around town. She checked with the police, the hospitals, the morgue. No one could help her. At week's end she returned to the village alone."

Listening to his grandmother's story, Wei suddenly imagined how horrible it was for his mother to be alone in Hong Kong. He wanted to find her immediately. The crowd began to scream as the ferry pulled in. Someone shouted that this wasn't the ferry at all but rather a mirage caused by the heat and the waiting. This idea forced a small laugh out of some others. The crowd moved closer toward the doorway. Wei's father was still asleep. Wei held his hand to his own heart and felt its rapid beats. He jumped up off the bench and watched the massive white side of the boat slide into place.

"Sit down!" Mai Wah cried. "We're not going anywhere yet. Don't get yourself all sick." Wei reseated himself on the edge of the bench again, and her eyes held him in place. "Years passed, and although the mother had already given up all hope of finding her son, periodically she returned to the city. There, at night, the beggars and the troublemakers would come out. It was especially dangerous then. In the dark she walked about, re-tracing steps engraved in her mind. Someone pulled at her shirt from behind. She turned around to find the horrible sight of a beggar, dark and dirty. He moved toward her, his arms braced on crutches. 'Help,' the beggar cried. She could not keep herself from backing away as she peered through the darkness. 'Help! It's me,' cried her son."

The doors swung open. The arriving passengers hurried down the gangplank only to be stopped by the sweating, waiting mass. No one could move. "Remember, Wei, every day in the big city, children are kidnapped and forced to beg. They are beaten and crippled so they will fetch a larger pot."

In his mind Wei heard his lost mother's voice calling him. He stood up and tugged at his grandmother's shirt. He wanted to hurry on board.

"Lin, Lin," Mai Wah called, "wake up. Let's go." Lin slowly began to rouse from his sleep.

When his grandmother did not move, Wei stepped alone into the crowd boarding the ferry. His feet found the gangplank.

He forced himself through plodding legs and rocked across it. Once on board, he turned and looked over the side of the ferry. His grandmother still stood in the same spot, pulling at his father's arm to wake him. The disembarking passengers yelled at the anxiously ascending crowd. Wei called to her, but she did not hear him.

When Mai Wah had gotten Lin to his feet, she turned back to look for Wei. He was gone. She looked at the doorway and then up at the white side of the ferry and gasped when she saw her grandson already on board. Slowly Lin pushed past her and told her in a groggy tone to come on. He continued forward, for a second holding her wrist, then letting go. Everyone hurried past Mai Wah; alone, her movements grew frightfully slow. She watched her son walk over the gangplank to meet Wei. Grabbing the railing, Mai Wah steadied herself to step on the rocking gangplank. "Full! Take the next ferry!" the captain shouted. She felt her world slipping away from her and she forced herself to continue on. The gate clanged shut behind her.

"Wei! Lin!" she cried as they approached her. "Why did you leave me?" The ferry pushed away from the dock.

Wei reached out to take his grandmother's hand.

II

STITCHES

THE NIGHT before her mother's funeral Mom dropped a bottle of Wesson oil on her foot. She had been refilling a small Pyrex shaker bottle that was kept conveniently on the stovetop for Dad's quick seasoning of Chinese food. Mom could not cook, not even an egg, but she cleaned with a fury. A bloody bone protruded through the skin. It was hard, wet, and had the shine of fine china.

Dad pulled up a pair of dirty trousers from the bathroom hamper and searched for his car keys. "I can't find them."

Julia and I ran into the kitchen. "What was that crash?" we asked.

Mom propped her foot up on the kitchen stool and wrapped it with a clean dishcloth. A red spot instantly formed from beneath the cloth. "How did I drop it?" she asked herself. "It's like someone pushed it out of my hand."

We followed Mom, who limped out of the apartment.

Behind us, Dad, jingling his keys, screamed, "Hurry, hurry!"

Mom sat in the front seat, tuning the radio to a music station. I leaned over from the back to listen. Mom lifted her foot onto the vinyl seat and held the dishcloth. When her leg arched, the dress fell to reveal the bowl of her knee which glowed white in the street light. The red spot on the cloth expanded.

Dad hopped into the driver's seat. "I had the wrong keys." He looked at Mom. When she ignored him and looked only at her foot, he looked at it, too.

"Just hurry," she said, "but get us there in one piece, okay?" Julia and I fastened our seatbelts.

Mom and Julia got off at the emergency entrance. It was the same hospital where Grandma had died the week before. Dad backed into an empty parking space in front of a brick wall. The rear brake light burned red. A crunch sounded as the seatbelt choked my stomach. "*Dil*—fuck," Dad said. He drove the car forward a little and stopped.

I unfastened the seatbelt and followed Dad out. He touched the back of the car and said, "The left light is broken. Maybe Mom won't notice it until after the funeral tomorrow."

The next morning, Mom came into Dad's and my room with a wet mop. I lay half awake under the sheets. "Get up," she said. "We're going to be late." With one eye open, I watched her foot. A thick cloth bandage was wrapped around it. It was clean and white. "Does it still hurt?" I asked her. "Yes," she said. She limped two steps across the room, set the mop down, pushed it forward with all her might and then pulled it toward herself again. The end of the stick touched her breast hiding under her T-shirt. She mopped every day. After several quick strokes, she held the tangled mop head upright and said again, "Get up."

Dad was already up. He looked uncomfortable in his black suit, the same he had worn when he had married Mom eleven years ago. But it was still a perfect fit. When he went off to work at the noodle factory, Dad wore T-shirts and jeans. When he sweated, his shirt stuck to his skinny body. He spent the morning loading up the station wagon with cardboard boxes of several varieties of noodles, including *chow mein,* a soft fried noodle; *sai mein,* raw and white, which had to be boiled and was served in a soup with roast pork and greens; and *e-mein,* an egg noodle, good enough to eat raw. Dad spent the afternoon dropping the boxes off at the different Chinese restaurants in Honolulu.

Last Saturday afternoon, before visiting Grandma in the hospital, I had helped Dad out with his deliveries. That morning, Mom took Julia and me to an outlet that sold Hawaiian shirts near the noodle factory. We picked shirts out from large cardboard boxes, competing with the Filipinas of the neighborhood. The women spoke their own language to each other, and sounded like chickens cackling. Mom claimed that they smelled, and lived off the government.

After buying matching Hawaiian shirts for Dad and me, Mom, Julia, and I had lunch at a Japanese coffee shop. Along with three *saimin*s, Mom also ordered her favorite shrimp tempura. She insisted as usual that the Japanese made the best shrimps.

After lunch, we still had an hour before I had to meet Dad for the noodle deliveries, so we took a tour of Pearl Harbor. A white lady in a U.S. Navy uniform explained what had happened on December 7, 1941, as she sailed the small boat out to the white fortress in the middle of the water. Aboard the *Arizona* Memorial, I read the names on the gold plaques. Mom stared over the side, looking at the sunken ship through dark sunglasses. It was big and rusty. "My father was in the navy," she said. "He died while stationed in Hong Kong." Every year she sent twenty dollars to a Hong Kong address so that a friend could buy flowers for her father's family plaque at the temple. I wondered if the person actually bought the flowers or kept Mom's money for himself.

It was getting late. Mom drove quickly to the noodle factory. Visiting hours at the hospital were beginning. "Come right away when you're done," she said, as she and Julia drove off to see Grandma.

Dad laid out a piece of cardboard for me to sit on in the station wagon so my shorts wouldn't be powdered white with noodle flour. Even during the day, roaches, some an inch long, crawled across the dashboard. Dad swore at them, slapping his hand down on the steering wheel. He drove fast when he made his deliveries. He wanted to get them over with. At the final restaurant we bought take-out and got a free bag of crispy wontons. During the ride to the hospital, I ate only one wonton, intending to save the rest for Mom and Julia.

We ate the take-out in the hospital waiting room, poking our wooden chopsticks into the white boxes. Before we finished eating, Mom got up and walked down the quiet white hallway. The beef *chow fun* holding her chopsticks upright turned cold. Full and tired, Dad, Julia, and I sat, waiting for Mom's return.

After a while Dad and Julia fell asleep, and I became hungry again. I started to pick out strands of brown *fun* noodles from Mom's box. Returning, Mom looked down at me as I ate her food. "All you do is eat and you never gain any weight, just like your father." She sat down on the edge of the sofa. Dad, with his legs spread open, snored.

The doctor came in, and Mom reached over me to hit Dad, to wake him up. They both walked a few steps away with the doctor and then stood still, listening to him. When they returned, Mom took the box of noodles away from me. "Don't eat any more. You're going to get sick." She pushed the box and chopsticks through the mouth of the silver trash can. "It's all finished. She's dead. It's time to go home."

Julia and I drove home with Mom in the family car, while Dad drove the station wagon alone. He drove fast, ahead of us. When the station wagon ran through a yellow light, I screamed, "Faster, Mom, faster. Don't let Dad get away."

"Be quiet," she said and stopped at the light.

The station wagon turned a corner and disappeared.

Sometimes after school Dad would pick up Julia and me in the station wagon. The factory's name and phone number were printed on its doors. After Julia and I had crowded into the front seat, I would tell Dad to drive fast, embarrassed at the thought of anyone seeing me in the dirty station wagon. Once when someone at school asked me if my father worked at a noodle factory, I answered that he owned one.

AT THE front of the funeral parlor we sat beside the coffin and flowers. In the first row of the congregation Auntie Vickie sat with a couple of workers from Mom's chop suey house. I loved Auntie Vickie. She was stylish and owned a jewelry store. No matter where she went, she was always dressed up and wore lots of makeup. Once she told me that babies in China were never adopted. Parents had enough to do for their own kids; why would they want someone else's? She and Uncle Mo didn't have any children.

Mom claimed that Auntie Vickie and Uncle Mo cheated at mah-jongg. "I don't want to play with them anymore," she said to Dad one night driving home from an evening game. "They cheat all the time and you never say anything to them about it."

"We're not sure they cheat," Dad said.

"I'm sure. Your cousin touches her eyes over and over again when she plays," Mom continued. "Is she afraid of her eyeballs falling out? I'm trying to figure out what it means. I think it means that she needs a bird tile or maybe a flower one. I'm not sure. Maybe they change the code for each game. When I find out what this means," Mom scratched her forehead, "I'll screw them over so badly they won't know what hit them." And then Mom added, "Mo Heng seems to have stopped talking about having kids. I bet that woman's barren."

In front of the coffin, the priest, wearing a black dress, spoke in Chinese and then in English, calling Grandma *Lauren*. Beloved Lauren. Beloved mother and grandmother. Lauren was Chinese. Auntie Vickie told me once that Mom did not look like Grandma. She did not even look pure Chinese. Her eyes were too round and had folds of skin above them. Her skin was lighter. Mom was also several inches taller than Auntie Vickie. But when anyone asked Mom, she told them that she was only Chinese. Nothing else. She had been raised in Hong Kong, had married a Chinese man, and had Chinese babies. "Three of them," she joked, referring to Dad as her eldest.

After the service, Auntie Vickie and I held hands and walked to the car. Its antenna held a tiny white flag with the word FUNERAL printed in blue letters. We got into the back seat.

Through the back window I watched Mom and Dad standing at the rear of the car. Julia got into the front. Mom was pointing at the broken taillight. I could hear Mom through the glass. "Didn't think I would notice," she said. I stuck my head out the window and watched her hobble to the front door of the car. She wore a black sandal over her bandaged foot. Her black dress was made out of Chinese silk; snap buttons held it together, extending from the high-neck collar to the end of the dress at the knees. "What's your mother yelling about now?" Auntie Vickie asked me, snapping open her paper fan with a quick flick of her wrist.

Our car followed the long black limousine into the street. The cars with little white flags attached to their antennas followed us away from the funeral home.

"So when are we playing mah-jongg again? This weekend?" Auntie Vickie started.

"I remember when my father died in Hong Kong," Mom began.

Auntie Vickie rolled down her window. The traffic noise drowned out Mom's voice. When Auntie Vickie's hair began to blow about, she rolled the window back up.

Mom spoke louder. "The night before my father's funeral, my mother cooked a large meal for all the relatives and a few friends. We burned incense to keep the bad spirits away from my father's body in the other room. A person's spirit is not safe until after the body is buried. My mother set some food—a bowl of rice, some pork, and an orange—in front of the white goddess. My mother was very much afraid of evil spirits. That night I slept with her in her bed. It was August, and hot and sticky in Hong Kong. The fan rattled warm air. I couldn't sleep. I perspired all over. My mother seemed to have dozed off. I got up to go to the bathroom. While I squatted over the hole I saw my father. He was shaking his head at me as if I had done something wrong. When I returned to bed I woke my mother up. Even before I told her what I saw she screamed, holding onto me. She was sweating and crying and all I wanted was for her to let me go."

It seemed that I was the only one listening to Mom's story. She had told this story many times before. Dad's father, Lin, had died last year. One day he received a letter in a blue envelope from Hong Kong. Chinese scribblings went up and down on the sheet. Attached to the letter was a clipping from a newspaper. The photo in the clipping was of an ugly old Chinese man with large ears and a very long face. I memorized the old man's face and then went to the bathroom to look in the mirror, wondering if my face would grow long and my ears large. I hoped that when I grew up I would look like Mom instead. But when I did something bad Mom would tell me that I was not her real son and that she wished that she could return me to the garbage can where she had found me.

The funeral procession drove into a tunnel through a mountain and came out the other side into a wet, green valley. A smaller mountain emerged and the black limousine ahead curved with the road in a slow, continuous turn. It began to drizzle. Dad and Auntie rolled up their windows all the way, while Mom and I stuck our arms out, feeling the cool rain and wind. Mom smiled at me in the rearview mirror. But when it began to rain harder we too were forced to roll up our windows.

It began to feel stuffy in the car. Auntie Vickie called to Dad in the front seat. "Guess what, the Canton opera is coming to town. Remember when we were little and wondered what the opera was like—the real operas in the theater, not the store-front ones performed by beggars every night?" She turned to me. "Our families were very poor when we were little. Too poor to go to the theater."

"I remember the operas in Hong Kong," Mom began. "Everything was so beautiful. The costumes, the stage, the actors. My mother would buy tickets weeks in advance. Sometimes we even got new dresses for the occasion. I always looked forward to those evenings. I want to go to the opera this weekend again."

"I'm going this Wednesday night," Auntie Vickie said. "I don't know if there are any tickets left."

"I'm getting hot," Julia piped up.

"Oh, by the way, Marie," Auntie Vickie continued, "did you get that job at the new dim sum restaurant in the mall?"

"Yes."

"Congratulations. The tips should be better than that old chop suey house. You're moving up."

Mom rolled down her window a little, and I felt relieved by the cool air rushing in.

The limousine turned into the roadway of the Kaneohe Memorial Park. Vases and pots of flowers decorated the hilly landscape of the park, carved up by black roads. On top of a small hill the limousine pulled over, and the procession of cars came to a stop.

It began to rain again. For protection the congregation crowded under a yellow tent. The sealed coffin sat in the rain, propped up over a hole in the ground. On top of the coffin the arrangement of red anthurium and white orchids glistened. Mom stepped out in the rain with an umbrella to examine how deep in the ground the hole was. She had told Dad once that the hole should be at least ten feet deep, or the body would be stolen by the evil spirits. Braced against the coffin, she kneeled down nearer to the hole, her black dress tight around her knees.

I was afraid of her falling in. But then she stood up again and walked back toward the tent. Her sandal slipped off her bandaged foot. I walked out in the rain to retrieve the sandal and brought it back to her. Under the tent she kicked her foot back into it. Gently she stroked my damp hair. Bits of wet grass stuck to her knees.

A cool breeze blew the rain under the tent, and the crowd moved closer together. The breeze smelled of plumeria flowers. Plumeria trees grew wild, clinging to the rising slopes of the mountains shrouded by clouds above. Plumeria were yellow, each with five velvet-soft petals. A poisonous white milk bled from the stem when ripped from the branch. Grandma loved plumeria. A small plumeria tree grew in her backyard. When Grandma was alive and well she would pluck flowers off her tree, soak them clean in a bucket of cold water, dry them gently on a beach towel, and string them together. She gave these leis to Julia and me to wear to school, two for each of us, extra ones for our teachers. After school, when Dad picked us up in the station wagon, only a few wilted plumeria remained on the leis. I set mine on the dashboard, an offering, hoping that the dying sweet smell would keep the roaches away.

While the priest prayed in Chinese, Mom whispered to Dad, "I want to go to the opera this weekend. It'll be just like Hong Kong. Get the tickets on your way home from the noodle factory tomorrow."

Not long ago in Grandma's house, I found a wedding photo of Mom and Dad. Mom holds a bouquet of orchids. The photos were stashed away in a soda cracker box at the bottom of a plastic garment bag smelling of mothballs. The day after she died, Mom and I went to Grandma's house. From that same bag Mom took out a black dress and, beside it, a wrinkled, yellowing wedding dress. She hung the black dress on the clothesline out back beside the plumeria tree. It stayed there for a week in the sweet breeze and the sun.

Sleepy, I leaned my head against the car window as we drove home from the funeral. With each bump on the highway my head knocked against the glass, creating oily smears. It was getting dark, and Mom's face faded in the rearview mirror. A hint of mothballs lingered from the front seat.

THE NIGHT of the opera Dad and I wore our matching Hawaiian shirts. Mom wore a new blue dress, which Dad zipped up in the living room. "Where did we get the money to buy all these new clothes?" Dad asked.

In Chinatown, we parallel-parked next to the open door-way of a pool hall. I peered in as Dad fed the meter. Filipino men played their games in the dark and smoky hall, their refuge from the pineapple cannery. Long fluorescent lamps hung low over the tables; the colorful balls shone. A few of the men were shirtless. Their ribs and shoulder blades jutted out from behind their leathery black skin as they twisted, turned, and bowed. Their lips held burning cigarettes. Smoke rose to cloud squinting eyes. The balls cracking against each other was even more deafening than the rattling of mah-jongg tiles. One ugly man spat on the ground, chalked his stick, and aimed to shoot again. Dollar bills and ashes fell off the tables. The man missed, slammed his stick to the ground, and swore.

In the Chinese theater, we all stared off at the empty stage,

surrounded by hundreds of Chinese people all speaking loudly
and with urgency, often gesturing with their hands.

"I want to go to Hong Kong and see my mother," Dad
began. "She won't be around much longer."

"Then you should go back," Mom said.

"We don't have the money."

They had this same conversation now and then.

Mom read the opera program and ignored Dad. She was
immune to his longing for his family in Hong Kong. Once, for a
school report, I had asked Mom about her own parents and
grandparents and great-grandparents. She had been ironing her
work uniform. Slamming down the iron, she looked at me and
said, "I was adopted. But don't tell your class that. It's none of
their business. Tell them about your father's family. He always
loves talking about them."

I told my class about Dad's childhood in China and how
his grandmother had fought off the Japanese during the war.
Once a soldier had punched his grandmother in the stomach.
(Dad usually told me this story after I had done something bad.)
Dad's grandmother risked her own life by first hiding him in the
shed where the rice was processed. But the story was different
with each telling. Specifics changed. The hiding place became
the attic, then the basement, then the outhouse. The Japanese
came in middle of the night, after school, during dinner.

I ended my oral report by telling the class that Dad came
to Hawaii and married Mom. The teacher, who was also Chinese, said that life must have been very difficult for my father
back in China. She mentioned the atrocities that took place during the Cultural Revolution, how the government killed people
for not conforming. On the map the teacher pointed to the
southern part of China, where Dad was originally from. "It was

very difficult and dangerous to leave China in the sixties. But if you did, you would've first escaped to Macao or Hong Kong. Was it dangerous for your father?" the teacher asked me. I nodded because I did not know.

In the theater, Mom brushed off her dress with the paper program. "I shouldn't have worn this dress. This theater is so dirty. You don't even know what's crawling beneath the seats. I'll have to wash this dress as soon as we get home."

Dad looked over at her. "You shouldn't have bought it in the first place. Maybe then we could save some money to go to Hong Kong."

"It's my money," she snapped. "If I want to buy a dress, I will. Save your own money to go to Hong Kong."

The lights went off, and the curtain rose. The zither music began softly and then increased in volume and tension to a sharp painful scolding, like Chinese people talking.

The stage lit up. It was a court in an old Chinese palace: oversized wooden chairs and dark wall panels, paper screens painted with flowers and mountains. The handsome young prince stepped onto the stage. His face was powdered white, and he wore a purple robe with wide sleeves. He moved tensely across the stage, raising his hands to his face. The music stopped and started, devoid of any rhythm. He sang a sad song, swaying his sleeves back and forth.

This was tonight's story: the melancholy prince is about to inherit the throne of the kingdom of China from his father, who had been seriously injured in battle. On his deathbed, the father reveals to his son that his mother is not the empress but rather a beautiful peasant woman who lives hundreds of miles away in the town of S———. The beautiful peasant woman had tended to the emperor's wounds during the last great war. The emperor asks his son to forgive him for taking him away from his true mother. After his father's funeral, the son leaves the empire in search of her. He finds her on a hilltop, hunched over and old, tending her vegetables. Her face is still beautiful. When the old woman sees her son, she sings a beautiful song. The prince carries his mother in his arms to the palace. But she is old and ill, and the journey tires her. The son dresses his mother in a long, flowing red gown and fancy jewels, and powders her face white like his own. But still she is not like the other members of the court; they disapprove of her peasant manners. In the final scene the old mother returns to her farm and dies in her son's arms.

Mom dried her eyes as the lights came on. Dad had already escaped through the exit door. Julia had fallen asleep. I watched the curtain fall upon the stage.

"Was it good or bad?" I asked Mom as we walked down the noisy, crowded street to the car.

"It was very good." Mom blew her nose. "It was very good."

"Look at your mother," Dad began.

Mom crunched her tissue.

"She cries only when it's not for real."

"Shut up."

The volume of their voices rose to compete with the shouts of the fat Hawaiian bar bouncers and the honking cars.

"But last week in the hospital, and at the funeral, she didn't cry. She didn't cry then." Dad walked faster, looking straight ahead at the car. "And now when it's not real, she can't stop crying. Isn't that ridiculous?"

"Don't say another word," Mom said.

"Silly woman."

Mom threw her tissue at Dad. "Shut up and leave me alone."

"Silly woman."

"Stop fighting," I said.

I felt a sharp slap on the back of my head. Mom had hit me. "Get in the car."

In the morning Mom came into my room with the wet mop. Dad had already left for work. I lay under the sheets. "Get up." She pushed the mop around the floor, anchoring the weight of her body with the bandaged foot. The bandage was now dirty. The stitches were coming out this afternoon. Mom carefully mopped every corner of the room.

"Get up or you'll be late," she said.

As she was about to leave, I called her back. "Mom, can I see the stitches before they come out?"

She looked at me in the dim light of the room. She seemed asleep. She turned on the small lamp on the desk, lighting up her eyes, large and red, her face white like an opera star's. She propped the mop against the wall, walked over to me, and lifted her foot up onto the bed. Gracefully, she unraveled the long gauze bandage. It swayed like a long, silky sleeve in a dance. I sat up and held the sheets over my naked chest. The bandage fell to the floor. Dark, brittle stitches held back the hard bone under the soft white skin.

FIFTIETH-STATE FAIR

ON THE evening of the Labor Day before Michael entered junior high school, his father took him to the Fiftieth-State Fair. An asphalt lot, converted overnight to a city of tents, housed pigs, cows, horses, and sheep. Booths offered both local foods such as *malasadas* (Hawaiian doughnuts) and *huli-huli* (charcoal-grilled) chicken, and American foods like hot dogs, hamburgers, and corn on the cob. There was also an assortment of games, the Land of New Products, and the brightly lit rides: the Ferris wheel, the colorful bumper cars, the Rock-n-Roll, the roller coaster. Father and son boarded the Caterpillar. Its convertible top moving on and off, threatening to decapitate the passengers as the ride circled, convinced them that this would be the most excitement for the money.

Michael smiled at his father and said, "I'm scared."

"Don't be a chicken."

Michael grasped the metal bar as the ride started up slowly.

"Ahh—" his father teased.

The ride sped up. One moment Michael was pushed up against his father, the next he was up against the cold steel side. When the top came down over them it became dark, and they seemed to circle faster. Michael felt he couldn't breathe. The ride seemed neverending. As they dismounted, he vomited onto the black asphalt. His father moved away from him.

Wei took his sickly son to a bench in the food tent. "Lie down here. I'll get us something to eat."

Michael lay down on the wooden bench. Above, thick poles stabbed up into the yellow canvas tent.

His father returned with a couple of bowls of *saimin* and a corn on the-cob. "Get up and try eating something."

Through the spaces between the wooden planks of the table, Michael could see his father setting down the partially eaten cob onto its red checkered cardboard plate. As soon as he attempted to rise, he spotted a few yellow teeth of corn littering the table, and then felt the tent caving in on him and his father while his chest rose to his throat. He lay down again.

"You're not going to eat?"

"I'm not hungry."

After a while Wei took hold of the untouched bowl of *saimin* and ate a few strands of the noodles himself. Then he declared it was too soggy to eat and a waste of money. He stuck the stringy gnawed cob into the bowl; liquid poured over the side and dripped between the planks of the table onto the ground. "Are you going to be sick all night?"

Father and son continued on a slow trek around the fair. They walked through the farm tent. The animals grazed lethargically on the hay-strewn parking lot. The smell of their feces made Michael want to throw up again. "Stink," his father agreed and they hurried out.

Next, the games. They stopped momentarily to hear a Hawaiian man, his T-shirt stretched over his fat belly and stained with carnival food, squeal with delight as he collected the pink elephant he had won by tossing white bracelets on red-tipped Coke bottles.

"What do you think?" his father asked him. "Should we try? Do you think Mom wants a pink elephant?"

"No."

"You're probably right. She only likes expensive things from the shopping mall. That's why we're always broke."

They shuffled into the final tent, the Land of New Products. At one table, a Japanese woman fried a new brand of Japanese noodles in a Teflon pan over a red hotplate. People crowded around for sample strands served in small paper cups. At another table, a white woman held to her neck a short black stick with a ball attached to its end. The ball jiggled against the woman's taut skin. Her red smile shivered with the movement of the Mini-Massager.

At the next table sat a long row of books, encyclopedias, each covered in white vinyl that looked like leather. Behind the books stood a white man with greasy gray hair, wearing gold wire-framed glasses. His green eyes stared at Michael from behind the glass. He had a popcorn-shaped nose. In front of the table were a couple of empty metal seats, which Michael quickly claimed. He lay down across them.

"Now this is what we can really use," Wei said. "If you

read all these books, you would be the smartest kid in school, go to a good college, become a lawyer or doctor, and make lots of money so you can support me later on, so I won't need to work at the noodle factory anymore."

How could a set of encyclopedias provide so much security?

His father weighed a book in his hands. "Knowledge and education are the key to success in any culture," he said, while hoisting it up and down as if it were a bag of gold. His hands caressed the rich white binding.

"A world of knowledge in each book," the white man said to Michael's father.

The edges of the books were stripes of gold. The pages seemed glued together and ripped noisily apart when opened. The salesman looked down at Michael lying on the chairs. "Too much roller coaster?" he said. "Just relax. Clear your mind." The man smiled. He handed Michael one of the volumes. It was *N*. "Open it," he said. "Look at the pictures. It'll make you feel better."

Michael sat up and fanned through the pages. He already felt a little better. His eyes settled on the heading *New York City*. Immediately he was transported to that other world: tall buildings, crowds, traffic jams, street-corner painters under a stone archway. An exciting world existed in a set of books. Each picture was a state fair. There in New York City, surrounded by so many people, one would never be lonely. At that moment, he knew he wanted to move there and to be among friendly whites.

The passing pictures in the encyclopedia reminded Michael of scenes outside a moving car. His nausea, the movement inside of him, magically transferred itself to the images in front of him. The world about him was in continuous motion; it moved even when he stayed still, like riding the Caterpillar. This realization calmed Michael down; it had never been his total responsibility to keep everything in motion.

He felt his father peering down at him, into his secret world, pulling him back to nausea. He closed the book, ran his fingers along the gold edge, the lock of the pages.

"Do you like them?" Wei asked. "Will you read them?"

"Yes," Michael answered.

The white man smiled. His teeth were yellow, and white hairs sprouted from his nostrils.

"If I buy them for you, will you read each one until you're smart?"

Michael nodded again.

Wei gave the white man his credit card.

"They'll be delivered to you in six weeks," the man said.

Michael could hardly wait.

MICHAEL AND his father stepped in front of the Ferris wheel. "That other ride made me a little sick, too. But I feel better now," his father said. "Do you want to go on this ride? It looks like fun, doesn't it? We'll go up so high. It doesn't look too bad, does it?"

"I still don't feel well," Michael admitted in shame.

His father's eyebrows crinkled and his eyeballs moistened. "Oh," his father said, disappointed.

The big wheel scooped up passengers, smiling and laughing. The wheel's light burned gaily. Michael saw himself and his father riding, their arms reaching up to the starry sky, as they looked down at the fairground and the city below. Everything would look miniature, as in a photo. For a moment, Michael thought he felt well enough to ride.

Then he heard his father's voice: "Why are you always sick? Why do you have to be like me? Why can't you be strong?"

THE CHINESE BARBER

MICHAEL SAT on the far edge of the sofa in the hair salon so that he could see his mother with her hairdresser. He enjoyed the smells of shampoo and aerosol hairspray. A magazine full of pictures of women's hairstyles lay in his lap. He preferred the hair salon in the mall to the barber shop in Chinatown where an old Chinese man smelling sweet and pungent, like tiger balm ointment, would cut his hair. His mother's hairdresser had blond hair and white skin and always wore black. He glided around her, a shiny pair of silver scissors in his right hand, a tiny black comb in his left. He lifted and cut off wet, dark strands of hair.

"You have such beautiful hair, Marie," said the hairdresser to Michael's mother, who looked only at her reflection in the three-way mirror lit up by hot white bulbs. "It layers well for cutting. I think we should make it short today. It has a wonderful natural body. How about short like that woman's?" The hairdresser pointed to the magazine that lay open on her lap. Her hand escaped from under the bib, revealing the sleeve of her restaurant uniform as she touched her hair. "Oh, no, can't do it. Not this time," she said. "Not today."

"Someday I'll get you to do it," the hairdresser said. "Everyone is cutting it short these days." He snipped off another piece of her hair. "Is that your son?" He pointed with the comb at Michael, who turned his gaze away from them. "How old is he?"

"Fourteen."

"You look too young to have a son that old."

Sometimes Michael imagined that the hairdresser looked in his direction, admiring his own black hair, so like his mother's. Michael wondered if the hairdresser would say that his hair, too, would be beautiful for cutting.

NEXT DOOR to the hair salon, Michael's mother studied the reflection of her hair in the glass door of the Chinese restaurant. She stood there admiring the way it had been styled. A little hairspray held it in place. She didn't seem to be in a hurry to go into the restaurant. She looked at her watch, reached into her purse, pulled out a ten-dollar bill, and handed it to Michael. He watched a dull expression come over her face as it faded from his sight past the glass door.

For a moment longer Michael stood at the entrance to the restaurant. He imagined his mother at work there. She would push a heavy silver cart, a rolling cafeteria, up and down the aisle. The carpet of the dining-room floor inhibited the smooth flow of the wheels. The steam from the straw baskets in the cart would melt away the sweet hairspray from his mother's stylish cut. She would answer the rude shouts of her Chinese customers, who called to her when she was still several tables away. For the ignorant white tourists she lifted the lids of the small baskets, each containing three dumplings, repeating over and over in her broken English what they were. She would return again and again to the kitchen to refill her cart. Michael imagined his mother sighing at the blurred reflection of her face and her messy hair in the silver tray at the bottom of the cart.

He held on to the wrinkled ten-dollar bill. It had been a part of his mother's tip money, and had probably lain on a wet, dirty table in the restaurant before she picked it up. He would meet his mother here at the glass door at the end of her shift at two o'clock.

He began to walk around the mall, wondering how he would spend the money. Though he had eaten only a bowl of cereal in the morning before they had set out, he decided to skip lunch and wait for the restaurant leftovers his mother would always carry home in a white take-out box. That way he could spend all his money shopping. A couple of Saturdays ago Michael had made the mistake of having lunch at a coffee shop in the mall, ordering a special that came with coffee and dessert. The check came to six dollars and fifty cents, and he left fifty cents as a tip for the Filipina waitress. She looked tired. Strands of kinky black hair escaped from the fishnet tie around her head. She looked older than his mother but probably wasn't. His mother had told him that Filipinas aged more quickly because they were poor and didn't take care of themselves. She looked at the fifty cents Michael had left for her. "You're not old enough

to work," she said. "I don't want your money." His hand shook
as he retrieved the two quarters. Embarrassed, he walked out of
the coffee shop, telling himself he would never eat there again.

IN AN hour he had walked around the entire mall, and at noon
he was hungry and tired. The thought of getting something to
eat depressed him. He sat on a circular bench surrounding a
group of palm trees in the sun, squinting his eyes, wondering
if he should eat and if so, what and how much of the ten dollars he should spend. If he had had a couple of dumplings
from his mother's cart, then he could continue walking around
the mall for the remaining two hours, shopping for something
to buy with all the money. He held on to the bill in his
pocket.

An older white boy sat down next to him on the bench.
The sun danced off the boy's short blond hair, greased back
with sweet-smelling gel. Michael thought he was a tourist because he wore a colorful Hawaiian shirt with his shorts. He
seemed to be looking at Michael out of the corners of his eyes.
The white boy turned toward him on the bench. "Shopping?"

"Yeah."

"You shop here a lot?" the white boy asked.

"I come here every Saturday."

"I love malls," the boy continued. "It's great the way
they're set up in Hawaii: the malls next to the beaches and the
hotels. And it's all outdoors too. Back in Chicago the malls are
all indoors. It gets pretty cold there during the winter. The other
guys from high school and I used to hang out at the malls together." He fell silent for a moment and then asked Michael,
"Bought anything today?"

"No," Michael answered. He thought this was a stupid question since he didn't have any packages.

"My name is Ronnie," the white boy said.

Michael told the boy his name.

"I bought this great magazine," Ronnie said. "Do you want to see it, Michael? It's called *GQ.*" He pulled it out from its paper bag and quickly flipped through it, tilting the pages toward Michael. It was like one of those magazines that he had looked at in the hair salon, but this one was exclusively for men. He watched the turning pages, feeling his heart pound faster because of the noon sun overhead, as he searched for the haircut that would best suit him. Ronnie held the magazine closer to him. The sun shone on the slanted final pages, revealing a photograph of a group of white men all with stylish haircuts standing on a beach wearing only bathing suits. His gaze froze upon them. His hands wanted to reach out to the magazine and draw it nearer to him for a more careful look. It propelled him into another world.

One Saturday alone at home, Michael had discovered a magazine on the top shelf of the hall closet. He took hold of it while his eyes memorized its exact position. In the magazine men and women wore only underwear. Some of the women were topless. He studied the shapes of their curving bodies and then turned these pages over. His eyes froze upon the next couple of pages. A group of white men stood together shoulder to shoulder, wearing only tight bikini briefs of different colors. Michael examined each one, but his gaze fell upon one man in particular. This man was unlike his father or any other Chinese man he'd ever seen without his shirt on; the man in the magazine seemed stronger and bigger. But most amazing to Michael was the brown hair racing all over his body, over his chest, entering into his briefs and reappearing on his thighs, a flow of hair that ended near his ankles. After a good part of the afternoon, he returned the magazine to the top shelf of the closet. But his eyes were not convinced that he had replaced the magazine in its original position. His shaking hands touched it, then took hold of it again. In a matter of minutes his mother would be returning home from work. But the imagined sight of the hairy man dared him to open the pages once more.

During the following few weeks, when he was alone in the apartment, he would return again and again to the top shelf of the hallway closet. Each time he returned the magazine to its former position he thought that its pages looked a little shabbier, a little more worn, betraying his secret.

Michael's eyes followed the movement of Ronnie's magazine as Ronnie returned it to its paper bag. Then he looked over at Ronnie's shorts pulled up at the side of his tanned legs. He studied the line that separated the dark and light parts of Ronnie's legs. His legs were further colored by tiny blond curly hairs. He wondered if hair, the same color as the hair on the top of his head, covered all of Ronnie's body.

"It's a great day," Ronnie said. "It's been beautiful every day since I've been here." He rested one hand on the paper bag containing the magazine while the other hand scratched his hairy legs. "Have you had lunch yet? I'm getting really hungry. I haven't eaten all day." He raised his blond eyebrows at Michael. "I know this place where we could get something cheap to eat. You want to go?" As he stood up from the bench Ronnie pulled his white shorts down over the tan line. "It's right down this way." He peered down at the boy.

Michael stared at the sunlight dancing off Ronnie's shiny hair as he remembered that he, too, was hungry.

IT WAS the coffee shop where the Filipina waitress worked. She wasn't smiling when she set down the menus on the edge of their table. Michael buried his face in the pages of his. He thought that she regretted having given back the fifty cents of the last time, and vowed to hide a larger tip under his plate this time.

The waitress returned to the table with two sweating glasses of water and took out her pad and pen. She didn't look at Michael at all.

Michael ordered a hamburger. He wanted some of his ten dollars back so he could buy a magazine to show his mother how he had spent the afternoon. He hoped to find the same magazine as Ronnie's.

After repeating "I can't decide what I want" several times, Ronnie ordered from the lunch specials, the part of the menu that was typed out and attached with a white plastic clip that told you to "Try Coca-Cola." A lunch special came with coffee and dessert.

"A hamburger's all you want?" Ronnie asked.

Michael told Ronnie only that he was in the eighth grade. He didn't feel that he could tell him any more. He didn't tell Ronnie about the Chinese restaurant where his mother worked or that he would have to meet her there in an hour.

Ronnie told him that he had been visiting the island for a few weeks and he'd had a hard time meeting Hawaiians. He wrapped his hand around his glass of water. Michael stared at the soft blond hair racing up from his hands to his arms and disappearing into the sleeves of the flower-print shirt. Ronnie asked Michael if he'd lived in Hawaii all his life.

He answered yes, but what he really wanted to say was that

most of the time it didn't matter that he lived here. The warm weather and how beautiful it always was—none of that seemed to matter. He couldn't compare Hawaii to anywhere else because he hadn't been to any other place. When he saw on TV or read in the encyclopedia how white people lived on the mainland, he imagined being somewhere else for a while. Maybe he would like it better than Hawaii and move to the mainland when he grew up.

"I love your warm weather," Ronnie said. "And beaches. I could live here for the rest of my life. I'm from Chicago. It's freezing there during the winters. The summers are hot and humid. Not nice like it is here all year round." He told Michael that the trip to Hawaii was a birthday present from his uncle, who had been with him for the first two weeks. But his uncle had to fly back early and had left him to spend the remaining few days alone. His uncle had a hair salon in Chicago. "I want to cut hair too," Ronnie said. "My uncle promised to set me up at the right schools when I graduate from high school. I can't tell my parents. They want me to go to college. My uncle cut my hair in the bathroom of our hotel room the day before he left." He twisted his head left and right to show Michael.

"I like it a lot," Michael said. "I want to get my hair cut at a salon. There's one here at the mall." He didn't tell Ronnie about the Chinese barber.

"I've walked by it a few times and admired the mirrors, the red bibs, the silver fixtures, the bright lights, the way the stylists here in Hawaii dress. They're all very chic. I've learned a few tricks from my uncle."

"My mother gets her hair cut at the salon."

"Oh, she does?"

It was one-thirty, the latest that Michael had ever eaten

lunch. He drank all of his water and began to chew on the ice before his hamburger arrived. He would have to go to the bathroom soon. He felt Ronnie's sandal fall on his foot, which made him pull his legs toward himself, rubbing them against the bottom of the vinyl seat of the booth. The back of his legs touched dried chewing gum and the sticky residue of previously spilled meals.

The Filipina waitress carried over their food, balancing the plate with the hamburger dangerously on her wrist while holding the plate of chicken à la king with her fingers. Ronnie asked her to refill Michael's glass. She picked up the glass, which left behind a small circle of water on the table. The waitress's hair was a mess under the fishnet. She looked even older than the last time, Michael thought. Silver hairs mixed with her black hair. He didn't really want any more water at the moment but knew that he would after he had finished his hamburger. He liked the fact that Ronnie was looking out for him.

"Thanks for having lunch with me," Ronnie said. "I've been eating here by myself for the past few days. That waitress probably thinks I don't have any friends."

Michael looked over at Ronnie as Ronnie ate his lunch. He also hated eating lunch alone on Saturday afternoons at the mall. Sometimes he had been too afraid even to order a hamburger from McDonald's. When he had, he would eat it quickly on a bench in the mall somewhere away from the crowd. Afterwards he would continue to walk aimlessly, never staying in one spot long enough to appear to be alone. Often instead of having lunch he would go hungry and imagine the leftover dumplings his mother would hold in the white box. He would eat them during the ride home.

He wanted to ask Ronnie if he'd had dim sum at the Chinese restaurant but knew that that wasn't the kind of place where you could eat alone, especially if you were a white tourist from Chicago. He imagined Ronnie and himself having lunch there. His mother would bring them the freshest and tastiest dumplings and pastries. Ronnie would be curious about all the various foods, as a typical white tourist was supposed to be, and Michael would patiently explain what each one was to him. But he saw his mother giving him and Ronnie an impatient look. She freed the hot baskets with her red and sore hands onto their table and hurried down the aisle pushing her silver cart. She had other customers to tend to. Michael imagined his mother's back moving away from him.

He bit into his hamburger while Ronnie ate his chicken à la king. "You have nice hair," Ronnie said. "I think it'll cut well. There seems to be a natural body to it. My uncle taught me what to look for in hair."

Michael reached up to touch his hair with his greasy fingers and thought of his mother staring at her own hair in the three-way mirror at the salon. She had a happy expression on her face. "What hotel are you staying at?" he asked.

"The Ilikai. My room has a great view of the beach and Diamond Head."

The Filipina waitress set the check down in front of Ronnie. Michael knew that his hamburger was $2.50. He calculated that he should get back $7.50 from his ten. He would leave the waitress $1.50 under his plate. That would leave him with $6.00, enough to buy the magazine to show his mother how he had spent the afternoon. It was almost two o'clock.

Ronnie placed his hand on top of the check, and Michael felt Ronnie's soft hairy legs touching his legs. Michael pulled his own legs away, backing them into the vinyl seat. But then the stickiness of the seat forced him to move forward, rubbing up against Ronnie's legs again. They tickled him. "I'm taking care of this," Ronnie said, picking up the check. Michael reached into his pocket and held on to the ten-dollar bill. He was glad he didn't need to spend any of it. It was moist from his constant playing with it. Ronnie reached into his own pocket and pulled out a ten and set it down on the table.

"I think you have to pay at the register," Michael said.

"Okay," Ronnie said. "In a few minutes. I want to sit and relax here for a little bit. I guess the waitress didn't bring you more water."

Ronnie looked toward the kitchen door for her. "Do you want my water?" He pushed his glass forward. "I just don't believe in eating and running. You're allowed your time in a restaurant. You're paying for being able to sit down. Besides, there aren't any customers at the door."

He hadn't meant to rush Ronnie, but it was getting dangerously late.

Ronnie continued to look at Michael's hair. "You have beautiful hair. I would love to cut it."

Michael reached over and took Ronnie's glass of water from his hands. He preferred Ronnie cutting his hair to that old Chinese barber in Chinatown. The Chinese barber never talked to him, as his mother's hairdresser talked to her or as Ronnie would talk to him. He thought that he would tell her that he had spent the ten dollars on a haircut. But ten dollars seemed like too much to spend on a haircut compared with the four dollars the Chinese barber charged. And besides, his last cut had only been a couple of weeks ago, not the five weeks he would let go by, while his hair grew thick and wild, before his mother would take him again to the Chinese barber.

Not long ago his mother had left him stranded in the barber shop while she did her shopping on the streets of Chinatown. It was not at all like the hair salon at the mall. The barber shop was dark, and its corners stacked with Chinese newspapers and magazines. On the counter, incense burned in a small gold cauldron. White ashes fell onto the strands of cut black hair discarded on the floor. The sweet white smoke clouded up the smiling Buddha statuette next to the pair of scissors and the hand mirror. Michael sat in a tall chair, his legs not reaching the floor. The Chinese barber forced him to look downward. The sharp blade scratched against the back of his neck, and the barber's bony hand gnawed at his head. Loose pieces of hair made him itch. Michael was forced to stare at the dirty edge of the wall covered with hair. When the barber let his head free for a moment, he looked quickly at the doorway, searching for his mother. But in a moment the barber forced his head down again. At the end, the Chinese barber held up a small hand mirror to him. He could barely see his face in the glass. Afterwards he sat in silence in a folding chair near the door of the shop, holding onto the safety of a magazine while his mother took her time. He scratched the back of his neck as he watched Chinese men come in for short haircuts identical to his. The barber spoke Chinese to them. No one talked to Michael. He began to wonder if his mother would ever return.

Michael knew that he had to get out of the coffee shop immediately. If he were late, his mother would be angry because she hated being at the restaurant a minute longer than she had to be. He looked again at the check ready to be paid. The food was eaten, the napkins crumpled. The vinyl seat burned his thighs.

"My hotel is not far away from here," Ronnie whispered. "I can cut your hair in the bathroom. I have the magazine, and you could pick the best cut out of it, and I'd do it just like the picture, like my uncle did for me."

Michael looked longingly at Ronnie. He wanted him to cut his hair. He wanted Ronnie's white hands massaging his scalp as he listened to the sharp, beautiful sounds of the clipping scissors flying around his head, his black hairs falling onto the protective bib. "You have such beautiful hair," Ronnie would say over and over. Ronnie would caress his stiff skinny neck, brushing away any tiny hairs caught in between his shirt and skin.

"Well, what do you say?" Ronnie asked. He leaned over the table. Beneath it, his legs wrapped around Michael's.

Michael could not answer and instead abruptly stood up, his sweaty thighs ripping off the seat. "My mother . . ." he muttered. Ronnie's eyes held onto him.

"Where you going?"

"I have to go to the bathroom."

"Okay," Ronnie continued. "The waitress keeps staring this way. It's making me nervous. Maybe she thinks we're trying to leave without paying. I don't think she likes me."

Michael looked back to see the waitress staring suspiciously at him too. He turned back to Ronnie.

Ronnie picked up the money and the check and stood up. "I'll tell you what. I'll pay the check at the register now, like you said to, and you go to the bathroom. Then we'll go." He counted out the money. "I don't have enough to leave her a tip. Got any change?"

The ten-dollar bill, Michael thought sadly. He reached into his pocket and handed it over to Ronnie.

"What's this?" Ronnie said. His mouth hung open as he stared at his hand as if his fingers had been cut off.

"That's all the money I have."

"It's half a bill." Ronnie's hand shook as he held it up.

Michael quickly pulled out the other half. "I can't go with you." He placed it in Ronnie's hand.

Ronnie closed his hand over Michael's. "But I want you to."

"I can't." He attempted to pull away. "I have to meet my mother!"

"Okay. Stop shouting." He looked sorely at Michael before letting him go.

Michael turned and walked to the bathroom. His heart was beating rapidly with fear that Ronnie would follow him in. When he reached the door, he turned around and saw Ronnie standing beside the Filipina waitress. She was holding the two halves of his ten-dollar bill. Ronnie hurried past her out the coffee shop, without ever looking back at Michael.

In the bathroom mirror Michael combed his hair with wet hands. His heart beat madly as he imagined his mother being angry with him. She would smell like cigarettes and Chinese food, and her newly cut hair would be a mess. In the car she would take a small comb out of her handbag and in the rearview mirror desperately attempt to restore it. She would ask him what he had done at the mall, how he had spent the ten dollars. He would force himself to eat one of her leftover dumplings, the cold salty taste mixing with the hot stuffy vinyl smell of the car in his dry mouth. He would feel nauseated from eating it too quickly while the car made frequent jolts because his mother never braked smoothly. He disliked being so close to her in a hot car.

Outside the bathroom, in the dining room, new customers sat at his table. The waitress held a brown paper bag under her arm. When she wrote on her pad, the magazine slid out onto the ground. Everyone looked down at the exposed pages.

Outside the coffee shop Michael stood alone. He knew he had to hurry. He told himself that his mother would not leave without him. He stared at the pavement as he ran as if someone were forcing his head down. He closed his eyes as he did when the Chinese barber cut his hair. Tears formed under his eyelids, caused by the loose hairs that the Chinese barber carelessly let fall into Michael's eyes.

A NICE CHINESE GIRL

WEI MET Marie in 1967 in an ESL class. Wei, twenty-four, had been in Hawaii for less than two months. After class he asked her to go with him to the Japanese coffee shop across from the high school. She accepted his invitation but insisted that in order to remain true to the spirit of the ESL class they could converse only in English. "It good practice," she added. She was repeating the beginners' level because she was secretly afraid of advancing and possibly becoming the worst student in that class, as Wei was. He always had to repeat the teacher's words several times before she gave up on him.

In the Japanese coffee shop foreign words fell like bombs. Wei grew frustrated: he would never figure out in English how to ask Marie to the movies. He leaned over the table to listen to her chopped-up English words. She was not speaking quite correctly, but he did not know how to begin to correct her. In fact Wei's number-one reason for taking the class was to meet a nice Chinese girl willing to share with him the challenges of living in America. He dreamed of someday opening his own Chinese restaurant. Work would not be a chore when you worked for yourself, he had concluded. Marie would be able to help him: with her command of English, she could play hostess to his cook. In addition to Chinese customers, they could attract American customers—and American money. Marie was easily the best-looking woman in the class, besides being the only Chinese one there. It would be good for business to have a pretty woman greet your customers. But still, up close, under the scrutinizing fluorescent lights of the coffee shop, there was something odd about Marie's appearance: she did not look *pure* Chinese.

"What—good—here?" Wei forced these English words out of his mouth.

"Everyt'ing. Eat *hambugga?*" Marie pointed to the table across the aisle.

A local man was eating one. Black meat between white buns. It would be a long time in America, Wei knew, before he could eat one of those.

"Me having *saimin*–shrimp tempura combo. Japanese make good shrimps."

Wei decided on a hot bowl of *saimin*, too, Japanese noodles, but without tempura. It was the closest thing to Chinese food. The air conditioner above blew cold air away from him into the center of the dining room; he began to sweat.

"Put menu down," she ordered, "or they won't come take order. They slow here."

The waitress arrived, a young, tanned Japanese woman.

"*Saimin*—shrimp tempura combo," Marie said. Her words sounded rehearsed. "Put shrimp on side. Don't want soggy in soup."

The waitress looked at Wei.

"Nu—dos," he mumbled. "Si—men." He pointed meekly to the table across the way.

She turned to look back and then asked, "Large or small?"

He had no idea what she was saying. "Si—men," he repeated. He felt too embarrassed to look at Marie.

"*Di, sai?*" Marie asked him.

"*Di!*" he blurted.

Marie grinned at the waitress. "Big." The waitress left.

Wei started up in Chinese, "But look at the *cha sui*, roast pork, in the soup. It looks stale. Leave it to the Japanese to copy us Chinese half-heartedly."

She responded in Chinese; he was no challenge for her English. "I like coming here because I work in a chop suey house, and I see and eat Chinese food every day. I'm sick of it."

How could she say that? "How is it where you work?" he asked.

"I don't like working. Period. But I've got to pay the bills and take care of my mother."

"Oh, yes." He sighed. Wei hated delivering Chinese takeout for his cousin's restaurant. "We all have to work," he said to Marie. He wanted to tell her about his dream of opening his own restaurant. But this dream seemed unattainable like the others. He was afraid Marie would greet it with cynicism.

"Someday I won't need to work. When money grows on trees. Ha!" She laughed.

The food arrived. Marie's shrimps did not look like shrimps; they were inflated and covered with a flaky yellow coating that seemed to disintegrate when she picked them up with her chopsticks. Between each bite, she sucked up several long strands of *saimin*. Wei did not like his big *saimin*. The soup was too salty: too much MSG. He sweated even more as he ate his noodles; he did not want her to think that he did not like them.

"Someday," Marie said, between bites of *saimin*, "I dream about running my own restaurant. I would serve real Chinese food, not the Americanized food they serve here in Hawaii."

He was so shocked by what she had just said that he unthinkingly picked up his bowl and drank his soup.

"It's the one thing I've learned," she continued, "how to run a restaurant. You only need common sense and, of course, money. How is it where you work?"

"Work is work. I work for relatives. The worst scenario," he muttered, wiping the salty sting from his lips.

"I can imagine," she said. "If you could open your own business without worrying about money, what would it be?"

"I guess a restaurant, too."

"Good." She smiled. She dropped her crumpled paper napkin with an air of finality into the bowl where it absorbed the remainder of the soup. "Did you like living in Hong Kong?"

"I hated it. Too many people."

"I love Hong Kong," she countered. "The shopping, the food, the theater."

He could not imagine what she saw in that hellish city. When father and son first arrived in Hong Kong they stayed indoors at a cousin's cramped apartment where they slept on the living-room floor. Then his father found a dishwashing job at a restaurant and left him home alone. When Wei found the courage to venture out he would walk slowly, along the inside edge of the overcrowded sidewalk. Perspiring profusely, he ducked into large, artificially aired stores to dry off; he touched every-thing in sight: shirts, pants, underwear, all wrapped in plastic. But then the scrutinizing looks of the professionally dressed Hong Kongese salespeople frightened him away. He discovered the sanctuary of the movie theater where he escaped to the mythical land of warlords and sword fighters. In one movie (the same one he wanted to take Marie to), a group of women war-riors led by their matriarch, a silver-haired woman with a pierc-ing stare who reminded Wei of his deceased grandmother, traveled through China. The women warriors stopped at a cliff where an old bridge had fallen down. There seemed to be no way to get to the other side. Suddenly the old matriarch raised her fist and commanded, "Human bridge!" The younger women warriors, all pretty and made up like Hong Kong women, pro-ceeded to climb on top of each other, feet to shoulder, their hands held their partner's legs above. The tower of women then lowered themselves like a drawbridge to the other cliff. The old woman warrior crossed over to the other side on the backs of her disciples. When she was safely across, the bridge came un-hinged, and the women slowly but efficiently climbed up on top of each other, until they were all, without a scratch, on the other side.

"Better food in China and Macao," Wei said to Marie. He set down his bowl to rest. Water dripped in from the air condi-tioner. Disgusting. He had officially finished eating.

"I've never been to China," she whispered.

He looked harder at her and realized that she was certainly not one hundred percent Chinese. She looked part white: folded eyelids; light brown eyes; long, softer hair; large, pointy nose; taller than most other Chinese women, even an inch or so taller than Wei himself. He suddenly realized he could never take her to meet his father. Marie would just confirm his father's belief that his son was up to no good, that he could never do things the way they should be done. But still Wei wanted to ask Marie to the movies. He would ask her in English.

"*Saturday — night — you want going movie?*"

Marie laughed. "It's *go*, not *going*."

"Why?"

"Because it sounds better that way," she said in Chinese.

"Stupid English."

"So what time Saturday *you want going movie?*" she asked.

"Saturday?"

"*Movie*, no?"

"Yes. Eight o'clock."

"Okay. I guess we'll take the bus."

"I'm sorry I don't have a car yet. But soon."

"We'll meet at the school at six-thirty, and take the bus to Chinatown and have some Chinese noodles beforehand. How's that?"

Outside Wei unchained his delivery bike and then walked Marie to her bus stop. "Maybe you should take the basket off before coming to class, or everyone will think you're delivering Chinese take-out." She giggled. The bus arrived and she waved goodbye and said, "Don't be late Saturday." He pedaled off.

Behind, the bus approached, and he imagined her telling the driver to run him over. As it passed he looked for her through the smoke-colored windows. What was wrong with looking like a delivery boy?

UNBUTTONING HER shirt in front of the bathroom mirror, Marie touched the small birthmark on her upper left arm: a dark, ugly raised island in a sea of white skin. Below it was a depressed scar, the size of a dime, from the vaccination she had received when she entered America. It was as deep inside of her as the birthmark was raised. She never wore sleeveless shirts because of the marks.

When Marie slept she dreamed about her *real* mother and father, not the adoptive parents who had brought her to Honolulu. In her dream, at thirteen, her real mother, the daughter of Chinese peasants, was sold to a brothel because her family's crops failed. Zhao Li (a name Marie made up) was held in high esteem at the brothel because of her extreme beauty. She was responsible for entertaining the warlords and the rich merchants. They loved and worshipped her. When they came they always brought her valuable gifts: Indian silks, fountain pens, ivory combs and brushes, English lingerie and lace, black round balls of opium in miniature jade jars. She made love to them routinely, as if she were doing housework.

After a while even the luxuries of the brothel could not satisfy her. She was stricken by a terrible depression that no amount of opium could cure. Instead, the drug numbed her to the violence beyond the stone walls: the wars, the revolutions, the riots, the invasions. Even the strange thunder of planes overhead did not frighten her.

One day a low-ranking white sailor arrived with no gifts. Normally he would have been directed to the back quarters where he could make love to a servantgirl behind a sheet partition. Zhao Li spotted him from her room, several flights above the ground floor's open central foyer. His stuttering and shaking brought tears to her eyes. She called for him. As he was brought up, floor after floor, his face widened with amazement. With his meager wages, how could he afford a woman so high up? he thought. The perfume of lotus and lily flowers intoxicated him. He stared with disbelief at the beautiful woman in front of him. Zhao Li offered him the pipe of opium, which he shyly admitted he had never smoked before. He giggled and coughed between sweet-tasting puffs. Nestling himself in the soft red satin of the bed, he watched her sing and dance, slowly removing her silk garments, before she stood trembling, naked, in front of him, her ivory skin glowing from the setting sun smoldering through the rice-paper windows. Her hands reached out to ruffle and then smooth his golden hair. She unbuttoned his stiff white shirt to discover skin as baby-soft as her own.

The war tore China apart. The white sailor never returned. In her mind Zhao Li envisioned him dying on his ship. Silver and red bombs fell from the heavens like stars and exploded on deck while he lay below in his bunk; he was dreaming of her. In nine months' time she gave birth to a beautiful baby girl. Her eyes were big and wide like his. One night the Communists incinerated the brothel, proclaiming it evil. Zhao Li escaped through the servants' entrance with her baby daughter and a small suitcase of valuables that she pawned along the way, from village to village. An old couple reminding her of her parents told Zhao Li to drown her baby in the river and to go to the country to be re-educated. She could be reborn in the new China, they said. Instead, one night Zhao Li took her daughter to a foreign hospital on the outskirts of town and left her there, hoping that she would someday grow up free and happy.

Marie imagined her real mother being sent to a re-education camp, where she was stoned to death for her selfish and lascivious past.

WEI WAS fifteen minutes late. He apologized profusely: he had had a last-minute delivery to make and had difficulty reading the street signs to find the address where he was to go. They spoke only a few words during the bus ride to Chinatown.

After first buying tickets for the movie, they went to the Chinese noodle shop, where he relaxed a bit as he watched Marie suck up her dumplings with the help of a soup spoon, as if she were being reacquainted with an old friend: before each bite she dipped a wet dumpling in red hot chili sauce, something you could never get in a Japanese restaurant. Then, both still hungry, they agreed to split a third bowl.

As they got up to leave, another couple sat down immediately after them. "In American restaurants," Marie commented, "they make you wait at the door while they clean up the table. Isn't that civilized?" "Yes, I guess," Wei murmured and then excused himself to go to the bathroom.

A line had already formed at the theater, rounding the nearest corner. They could not be assured of aisle seats. Marie fretted about having to sit too close to the screen or behind someone with a big head. Wei reminded himself to urinate again before sitting down, remembering the bowl of soup and numerous cups of tea he had just had. Chinese noodle soup was infinitely tastier than *saimin*. But still, he should not have drunk all that soup. When he was little his grandmother would curse him for wetting his bed, and now at twenty-seven he made himself go to the bathroom even when he did not really need to, afraid of not having an opportunity later. But how could he go again without giving the appearance that he had a bladder problem or was a worry-wart? He would offer to buy Marie some candy — some American candy: she would like that.

The line moved, and the crowd pushed them up against

each other. He noticed other men looking at Marie and then at him. I'm lucky, he thought.

Inside she agreed to M&Ms and then walked alone into the theater. Wei watched the crowd swallow her before he headed to the snack bar. After purchasing the candy, he sneaked off to the men's room, and at the urinal held the box of candy in his armpit as he pulled out his *googoojai*. It was nice to go to the movies with someone. He set the candy on the counter as he washed his hands. He wondered if Marie would go out with him again.

He felt happy as he walked into the theater, knowing that she was saving him a seat. His eyes widened to look for her in the dark. The place was full. He knew he should have asked her where she would be sitting. Slowly he walked down the aisle. What if he walked all the way to the front just to have to turn around to go back up, still looking for her? What if he never found her? The preview for a coming attraction passed in front of him. An arm shot up in the crowd, illuminated by the movie light. He pushed his way past legs. The familiar operatic zither music of the credits delivered a sweet pang of relief. "You didn't miss anything," she whispered. "The preview looked horrible." Comfortable silence descended upon them.

The first image of the movie appeared: the matriarch paced before her court, pondering out loud the attack on her empire by an army of evil men. The long jeweled case of the sword attached to her belt almost touched the floor. "The candy?" Marie asked.

"Oh," Wei gasped. "I left it in the bathroom." He looked at all the legs in a row blocking his path to the aisle. "I'll go back and get it."

"Oh, never mind, just watch the movie." As they watched,

he relinquished the armrest to her in order to avoid their touching. The empress on the screen decapitated a man with her sword. She leapt over bushes and into trees. But none of this, Wei knew, compared with the impending bridge scene or with the tension he felt while sitting beside Marie in the dark.

The bus ride back was shortened by the lack of traffic late at night. He asked her if she had liked the movie.

"It was all right," she stated. "But I didn't believe that human-bridge scene for a second. It looked fake. Too bad there's only one Chinese movie theater in Hawaii. You don't like American movies, do you?"

"It's not that I don't like them," he said, "it's just that I wouldn't understand what's being said. I like James Bond."

"Yes, me too. Lots of action and gadgets. So much so you don't really need to know what they're saying." They both laughed.

As the bus approached the spot where Wei's bike was parked, Marie pulled the cord to signal the driver. "I guess I'll see you Tuesday," she said. "Thanks for the movie and dinner. *I have good fun.*"

He did not believe her. He moved out of his seat, past her long legs and down the aisle to the exit door. When the bus stopped, he turned back and was surprised to see her waving and smiling at him.

He rode his bike in first gear. The pedals felt loose under his feet. He moved along slowly; he did not have to be anywhere in a hurry. There was no delivery to make; no one's food was getting cold. Pausing in his pedaling, he shifted to second gear. The pedals stiffened momentarily. He pushed hard and propelled himself forward. The houses around him were separated by mango trees towering and cutting across the starry sky of *Tan*

Hong San, the land of the fragrant mountains. He wondered if he was wasting his time with Marie. He hated her criticism of him and of everything Chinese—criticism, he believed, she could utter only out of jealousy because she herself was not pure Chinese. Why could she not be content with things as they were? The human bridge was believable enough. Sometimes you just had to believe. He cursed the bike for being so slow-moving. Again he resolved to save enough money to buy a car. That could be years from now. Everything moved slowly. But why was he always in such a rush? Only time would reveal whether Marie was the one. She laughed at everything. Could she take anything seriously? He knew it would never be easy. Did she have the patience to spend a lifetime with him? He was still unsure about her.

THE FOLLOWING Tuesday they found themselves in the coffee shop again. Wei asked Marie what was the saucy beef the people across the way were eating, and she explained it was beef teriyaki, *see-yo gno-yuke.* It looked tasty, he added, and decided to order it for himself. In class she had noticed how distressed Wei looked as the teacher came around the room with her English questions. Marie whispered an answer to him. He repeated Marie's exact words. The teacher smiled at him for the first time ever.

Over the weekend Wei thought constantly about Marie. She was sexy and he liked her drive: she was a woman who knew her mind, easily the best student in the class. Though the possibility of opening a restaurant together was still years away, they nevertheless shared a dream, which was very important. Man and woman cannot live together without shared dreams. He felt on the verge of accepting her American ways: he was in America now; it was time to adapt, and what better way than with an Americanized Chinese woman? But still, he knew his father would ask about her family's background.

Marie's big-boned hand pushed the menus to the edge of the table. They were sitting in a different booth; Wei could feel the cool breeze of the air conditioner. They were ready to order, and a pleasant silence fell between them as they waited for the waitress to arrive. It was busy as usual. For the first time, Wei noticed the Japanese garden out back, past a screen door. A small waterfall, soft and constant, trickled down coarse black rocks into a waiting shallow pool where orange goldfish swam. Gathered around the pond were a couple of expertly groomed *bonsai*, polished gray stones large enough for a child to sit on, and a miniature pagoda whose window emitted a romantic light. The beauty of the garden was only slightly marred by the water hose's end jutting out at the top of the waterfall. Marie sat with her back to the garden. "They're very slow here," she said sharply as she looked for the waitress. "There's a crowd at the door, and that table over there has been sitting dirty and vacant for fifteen minutes. That's how long we've been sitting here, too."

Wei searched longingly for the waitress. When he looked back at the garden, he could see dirt on the screen door, obscuring his view. He wondered how it would look in daylight. It would probably appear fake. The metal end of the hose would be rusty from the endless flow of water. He heard his father asking him, "But where in China is her family from? I hope she's not one of those obnoxious half-breed women. Remember, your mother, also an ambitious woman, left both of us."

"I want our waitress to come now," Marie declared. When

she raised her arm, her shirt sleeve crumpled down. Wei spotted the stubble of underarm hair and, on the other side of the arm, an unsightly dark mole. He returned his gaze to the garden. There was no room to play in it; you would risk being stabbed by a *bonsai* or knocking over the pagoda, whose only light was a meek yellow bulb.

Marie brought her hand back down on the menus. They threatened to fall off the table. The shirt sleeve slowly fell back in place, but not before Wei had seen Marie's vaccination scar, ugly like his own.

"Where is your family originally from?" he asked.

"I told you. Hong Kong."

"But no one is from Hong Kong," he insisted.

She stared coldly at him and in desperation lifted her arm again. The menus fell off the table onto the floor and slid irretrievably under another customer's chair. The waitress emerged from the kitchen, carrying a trayful of bowls. The waitress seemed to acknowledge Marie this time as she set the tray down on the edge of another table, and began passing out the hot *saimin*.

"It's just that my father would want to know," Wei pursued.

Marie, with her arm still raised, looked mutely at him. She realized this was how Wei must feel when he could not answer the teacher's questions. Had he already forgotten how she had helped him in class earlier that evening?

The waitress escaped to the kitchen. Defeated, Marie let her arm fall again. "She's not coming," she muttered. "I don't think we should stay any longer. It's hopeless."

"Maybe we should wait just a little longer."

When he did not move, she stood up and said, "Let's go."

He hurried behind Marie, who pushed forcefully past the backs of eating customers' chairs. As she walked by the kitchen, the waitress re-emerged. The Chinese waitress stared intently at the Japanese one.

"Me waitress too," Marie started. "We wait ten, fifte'n minute for you come." Her voice rose. "Me waitress too. Me don't let you wait long. That not how run rest'rant."

"We're very busy," the Japanese waitress replied, annoyed. "And this is not *my* restaurant. I only work here."

"Fifte'n minute."

"If you don't like it, you don't need to eat here."

Marie turned back to Wei, and she knew he would not help her. He could not even speak English. He was *mo yung*—good for nothing. She walked out.

He quickly followed behind.

She led the way to his chained bike. *What does it matter if I'm not pure Chinese? We're living here and now. That's enough for us to concern ourselves with. There's no good reason to look back. Nothing ever comes out of it.*

When he caught up to her waiting at his bicycle, she said, "It'll be a long time before I go back there. That's not how you run a restaurant. That's not how I would run my restaurant." He fumbled with the lock. As they walked, side by side, to her bus stop, the bike's basket rattled, and its pedal scraped against Wei's trousered calf. When he moved sideways, away from the bike, still holding and pushing it along, he found himself closer to Marie. She kept beside him. Occasionally their arms, possessing twin vaccination scars, touched.

SUMMER VACATION

MARY, BOB, and Jason are the first white people ever to move into the Laus' apartment building. Mary lets Julia and Michael sit with her as she feeds Jason. She smiles and giggles like a girl every time Jason drools out his food. Mary has blond hair and is the perfect mother. Each spoonful of food is round and looks tasty. She lifts the spoon to Jason's mouth and coos as if telling him to open wide and eat.

The four Chinese families (including the Laus) all live in the downstairs apartments. Upstairs live Mary, a Japanese family, a Hawaiian family, and a Filipino couple. Their Uncle Wang owns the building, and the Laus are the managers. They keep keys to all the apartments hidden away on the top shelf above the sink in a tin box that once held sweet, golden bean cakes reserved for Chinese New Year. The keys have been there forever. Michael wonders who ate the bean cakes. Once, when their mother and father were both at work, Julia and Michael took the box down from the shelf and took turns blindly closing their hands over one of the keys and guessing whose door it could open. But they never think about using the keys themselves. They know they're not supposed to go into other people's apartments without first being invited in. Their mother, Marie, occasionally tells the story of when baby Julia walked into a neighbor's apartment (people sometimes keep their doors open to let the breeze in) and urinated on the floor.

Mary is the first person in the building to *invite* Julia and Michael into her apartment. It's just like theirs downstairs, they think. But since Mary's apartment is upstairs, she has something very special that their apartment doesn't have: a lanai, outside the living room's screen door, where Mary can lie on her reclining lawn chair and tan in the sun.

"So your parents are from China?" Mary asks.

"Only our father," Michael answers.

Jason finishes up his food and Mary picks him up, puts him on her shoulder, and taps his back.

"And your mother?" Mary sets Jason back down in the highchair.

"I don't know," Michael says.

"She looks a little Hawaiian, you know."

Julia is not saying a word. She is mad at Michael for two reasons. The first is that they aren't supposed to talk about their family with other people; that's what their father told them when Michael asked him about growing up in China for his school report.

The second reason is that he wanted to go to Mary's apartment instead of staying with Julia, as usual, at the railing to watch the neighbors come home. They especially wait for Randy Domingo. It was in the Domingos' apartment that Julia had urinated.

Before Mary moved into the building, Julia and Michael would spend most of their time after school at the railing at the top of the stairs, looking down at the parking lot and waiting for Randy. Randy is in high school. They watched him park in the far left stall and walk into the building and up the stairs. Once Randy pulled out from the back seat of his car a white surf-board, which stood taller than him. He wore only a pair of Ha-waiian swimming trunks. His skin was dark and shiny. Sand covered his legs and feet. As he walked up the stairs, Michael and Julia saw that the arm that held onto the surfboard was stiff and strong. He smelled of coconut suntan lotion. They watched him stick the surfboard, pointy end first, through his apartment door. After Mary moved into her apartment, she saw Michael and Julia standing out near the railing doing nothing and invited them in.

Their father calls them to dinner, and Julia leads the way down the stairs, mumbling that she isn't even hungry. They eat earlier than other people because their mother starts her evening shift at the restaurant at six o'clock. Julia and Michael linger over their food until the rice is cold and sticks to their plates. They dislike most of all the vegetable soup, served toward the end of the meal. Their father scoops wet, dark green leaves into bowls with a little soup and pushes the bowls in front of Mi-chael and Julia, and they spend even more time eating the soup than the rest of the meal. Once it tasted so bitter that Michael went to the bathroom and spat the greens out in the toilet. He flushed it twice to make sure that they wouldn't come back up.

IT'S SUMMER vacation. No school. Julia and Michael get up and go up to the railing to watch their mother drive out of the parking lot to work. Their father has already left. They are still wearing the shorts and T-shirts they slept in, and their skinny bodies are like hangers for their clothes. The sun feels hot. They think their skin is yellow (since they're Chinese) and therefore doesn't tan as well as Randy's brown skin. Instead they turn red when they stay in the sun too long. They walk by Mary's apartment and look in, but the wooden door behind the screen door is shut.

They go back home, and before they climb back into their bunk beds, they rub a little Noxzema on the back of each other's neck. While lying in the top bunk Michael asks Julia below about what they are having for lunch. Their mother boiled some rice and told Julia to fry up some eggs and Spam. Before, Julia and Michael slept in different bedrooms. Their mother called their father lazy because he hasn't thrown away the bed (formerly Marie and Julia's bed), which is crowded in their bedroom a foot away from the bunk bed. "Next week," he always says. In order to get up and down from the top bunk, Michael jumps on the bed. An aluminum railing, its base inserted beneath the mattress of the top bunk, keeps Michael from falling to the floor in the middle of the night.

Julia and Michael wake up again at one o'clock, and Julia tells Michael to serve her lunch in bed. She begins to kick the bottom of his bunk and screams, "Sensurround!" Her lips rumble earthquake sounds.

Michael is trapped above. His bed shakes. "Help!"

"You're going to fall into the earth."

Michael buries his face in the pillow, feeling Julia's kicks through the mattress in his stomach. He starts to laugh, but then suddenly the bed moves awkwardly and one side begins to fall in. He feels himself sliding. He leans over the railing and jumps onto the bed below. Julia rolls onto the ground as the top bunk comes crashing down with a thump onto the bottom bunk.

They can't believe what has just happened. "What are we going to do?" Michael asks. "You broke the bunk bed. Mom's going to get mad at us. You better fix it. We might even get hit."

"I'm too old to be hit," Julia says. She gets up from the floor, rubs her head, pulls her shorts over her panties and begins to pull and push at the mattress. It doesn't move. Julia tells Michael to go and ask Mary to come down to help them.

Mary's wooden door is now open. Michael knocks on the screen door. The sun is pouring into her kitchen, lighting up her crossed white legs as she sits at the kitchen counter with Jason. "Hi, hi," Michael calls. "Hi," she says. "I'm feeding Jason right now. And I'll have to bathe him afterwards. Now's not really a good time."

Michael doesn't say anything at first and is about to go away, but then thinks about the broken bunk bed, and says, "We need your help. Both our mom and dad are out, and our bunk bed is broken. We need some help fixing it."

Mary doesn't say anything. She gives Jason another spoonful. "How did you break it?" she finally asks.

"It just fell. It's too heavy for us to put back together by ourselves."

"Bob," she calls. Bob's deep voice comes from inside the apartment. Mary comes out. "Now, how did you break the bunk bed?" she asks Michael again.

"Your apartment is just like ours," Mary says as she walks

in. Michael leads her to the bedroom. "There are so many beds in this room," she says. Julia stares at Mary's feet because she is still wearing her sandals, and everyone has to take their shoes or sandals off at the door. Julia and Michael grab one end of the top bunk while Mary holds the other end and they lift it back into place. Mary is sweating through her T-shirt. Her arms cling to the sleeves. She's not skinny like Julia and Michael. She sticks the railing back under the mattress. "I have to go and give Jason his bath," she says. "It's Bob's day off, but he is so tired. It's his first day off in eight days. We were going to go to the beach this morning, but he just couldn't get out of bed. I did get some sun on the lanai." She shows them her pink arms. "I better start using suntan lotion, or I'll turn into a lobster." Michael doesn't know what she means. They walk Mary out of the apartment. Julia checks for any dirt on the parts of the floor that Mary walked on.

ONE EVENING their mother starts work at the restaurant at four o'clock in order to set up for a special party. They won't eat dinner until later. Their father takes a nap on *his* plastic chaise longue out back. Julia and Michael go upstairs to Mary's and watch her comb out her long, blond hair, stroke after stroke. Julia also reads *TV Guide.* Jason sleeps in the other room. Mary asks them what she should make for dinner with a pound of hamburger. They don't eat hamburger because their father said that it is made from the leftover parts of the cow, all ground up together. Mary hands Michael a Hawaiian cookbook. He turns to the meat section and finds a recipe for teriyaki hamburger. He had it in school once, he tells Mary, and liked it. The recipe calls for a pound of hamburger.

In the kitchen, Mary takes out from the top shelf a bottle of Wesson oil and a bottle of soy sauce, not the brand that Marie gets in Chinatown but a Japanese brand that you can buy in any store. Mary then takes out the beef from the refrigerator, still in its plastic wrap. Michael peels off the wrapper and lifts out the cold, stringy meat. Mary doesn't have any sesame seed oil, and tells him to use more Wesson. She measures out the oil with her eyes, pouring the thick, silky liquid over his hands and the meat. Next, the soy sauce, black and salty. Mary turns on the oven. Michael's hands knead the meat and the liquid together. Julia sits and watches from the kitchen counter. Jason begins to cry from the other room. "Oh, no," Mary says. "It's time for his milk." She washes her hands and goes off to Jason. Michael mixes the meat a little more until all the liquid sinks into it and forms one large brown lump. He then makes small balls out of it and sets them in an aluminum pan. He washes his hands and opens the oven a crack to feel the heat blow on his face. Julia stares out the screen door, hoping that Randy will pass by on his way home. Michael starts to feel hot.

"We have to leave soon," Julia says. "We have to go and eat dinner."

"What about the hamburger?"

"We're not eating it," Julia says.

"I want to finish cooking," Michael says.

Julia tells him that he's not really supposed to be doing that.

Michael walks to Jason's bedroom. The door is almost closed. He walks up and pushes it open. There on the bed, Mary lies on her side with Jason in her arm, side by side. Mary's breast falls out of her shirt, white and fat and smooth, and Jason's small hands take hold of it, and he kisses it. "Oh, Michael," she says. She holds her shirt gently over her breast. "What about the hamburger?" he asks her. "Can I put it in the oven?" "Yes," she says, looking only at Jason. The shirt falls from her hand, and Jason still holds onto her breast, kissing it between each breath he takes.

Michael goes back to the kitchen; Julia is gone. Michael looks out the screen door and sees her holding onto the railing, looking down at the parking lot. Her skinny body shifts in her loose T-shirt as her feet pivot from side to side on the bottom bar of the railing. There is a soft, white crease of skin under her arm.

Back in Mary's kitchen Michael puts the pan of brown balls into the hot oven. Sweat runs down his forehead. The front door opens and Michael turns around, expecting Julia. Instead Bob comes in. He looks surprised. "Are you cooking dinner to-night?" He holds his shirt over his back, his skin is red, and his breast sags a little. Hair the same color as on top of his head comes out from his armpits.

Mary returns to the kitchen, all buttoned again, holding Jason in her arms. "Hi, Bob," she says and comes over and kisses him on the lips. "You're home early."

"Finished up a little earlier today."

"Michael is cooking tonight. Some kind of Chinese hamburger," Mary says.

"Smells great."

Michael doesn't tell her that teriyaki hamburger is Japanese. Mary gives Jason to Bob and then she cracks open the oven door a little. Jason lays his head on Bob's bare chest next to his nipple, but he doesn't kiss it. Instead, Jason drools out white spit. "Oh," says Bob. "You just feed him?" Bob's free hand smears the white spit into his chest.

When dinner is ready, Michael dishes out the hamburgers onto two plates and a smaller ball onto a small plate for himself. Mary scoops out carrots and potatoes onto her and Bob's plates only. "It looks delicious," Bob says. Michael finishes his small piece while still standing near the sink. Mary puts Jason in the highchair and gives him a small piece of meat from her plate.

Michael hears Julia call him. As he leaves he looks back and sees that in the light of the setting sun Bob's skin is red like a lobster.

"Dinner is almost over," Julia yells from their front door as Michael walks down the stairs. "You know you shouldn't have cooked their dinner. You're going to get in trouble."

"Why?" Michael doesn't say anything more but wants to tell Julia that they don't need to tell Mom anything about it, since they didn't say anything about the bunk bed accident. Michael wipes the teriyaki taste from his lips with the back of his hand.

JULIA SEEMS to wait longer each night before coming to bed. Michael lies awake on the top bunk, unable to sleep without her vibrations below him.

Ever since the top bunk fell through, Michael gets in the habit of touching the frame of the bunk along its cold, steel edge, feeling the bed secured in place.

When Julia comes to bed, Michael asks her, "What is Mom doing?"

"She's watching TV."

"What is she watching?"

"A police show."

"Were you watching too?" His hand begins to linger along the steel frame again.

"Get your hand away from my bed," Julia calls.

He pulls his hand away and does not say anything more to Julia. After a few minutes pass and he is still unable to fall asleep, his hand reaches below again. His fingers rest carefully on the crack between the mattress and the steel frame. Is Julia safe?

ONE MORNING at the top of the stairs, after watching their mother drive off, they see a small stream of smoke blowing out of the Domingos' front window. They walk to the door, which is shut. The smoke smells of something burning. They hear Mary's door open. "What's burning?" she asks, coming out. "Oh, no." She knocks on the Domingos' door. There is no answer. "They must have left something on their stove. Do you have the key for their apartment?"

Michael leaves Julia and Mary at the doorway and hurries back downstairs. He climbs up on a chair and into the sink, where he stands to bring down the box from the top shelf. The keys have a strange, dirty feeling, and his fingers instantly smell. He can't find the key labeled 7 and imagines the apartment building burning down. Finally he finds it, takes it upstairs, and hands it over to Mary. She opens the Domingos' door. Julia and Michael stand still at the doorway as the smoke rushes out past them. With a nearby dishcloth, Mary picks up the burning pot from the stove and places it in the sink. She turns on the cold water and smoke rises to the ceiling, the entire inside of the apartment turning heavenly white.

"We should leave the door open for a little while," Mary

says. "I have to go back to Jason. Just shut the door after a few more minutes." She goes back into her apartment and shuts the wooden door behind her.

Julia and Michael stand on the threshold of Randy's apartment. "What shall we do?" Michael asks Julia, who only stares ahead into the apartment, still thick with smoke. "Do you want to go back to bed? Do you want to have lunch?"

Julia takes Michael's hand and pulls him into the apartment. As they move further in, Michael becomes afraid that they will not be able to hear Randy on the stairs. As they stand in front of his bedroom, Michael wonders if Julia loves Randy. The surfboard leans dangerously against the side of a desk. It rises at a slant to the ceiling. Julia lets go of Michael's hand, walks up to it, and knocks on the hard surface. It sounds hollow. It rocks just a little. Michael walks up and touches it, waxy and smooth. Randy's bed sits off against the side where their bunk bed is downstairs. His bed is unmade, the sheets messed up with clothes, shorts, T-shirts, and crumpled white BVDs.

From the outside comes the distant sound of slapping sandals. Michael follows Julia quickly out of the bedroom and through the kitchen. Randy approaches them as they step outside of his apartment.

"What are you doing?" Randy asks sharply.

"Your pot was on fire." Julia begins to describe the scene with her hands and by blowing air out of her mouth. Randy steps into the apartment and shuts the wooden door on them. The key juts out of the doorknob.

ONE AFTERNOON they take a walk with Mary and Jason along the canal, a few blocks away. Michael pushes Jason's stroller while

Mary tells Julia how much more she likes living in Hawaii now. "When we first moved here from the mainland, Bob and I had a difficult time getting used to things. I felt that the people here were treating us differently. Bob complained about the guys he worked with. They never talked to him. I told him that we should give it six months, no more than a year. But now we're getting along fine. Bob has made a couple of friends at work. He plays cards with them. And I have a couple of new friends, you two. And Hawaii is *so* beautiful."

Michael is relieved that Mary likes it better in Hawaii and that she'll live upstairs for at least a year. That's how long the lease on her apartment is for. If Mary wants to get her deposit back when she moves out, she has to stay that long. If she doesn't, she'll lose the money. Michael thinks his mother decided to rent the apartment to Mary because she cared only about whether the tenants were clean and quiet and would pay their rent on time. "Look," Marie said to their father, Wei, one night before Mary moved in, "just because you're Chinese doesn't mean you'll be a good tenant. These white people have a good job. They look clean." But then if Mary and Bob move out before their lease is up, Michael doubts that his mother will say that again.

He pushes the baby stroller on the walkway beside the canal, which stretches out in front of them, its water dark green. Four high-school boys in a canoe, all dark-skinned and naked above the waist, paddle themselves past. The water rips apart at the tip of their canoe and folds around its waxy sides. An old Japanese fisherman under a straw hat, dressed in long pants rolled up to his knees, his body wrinkled and brown, holds out a skinny pole. A string attached to its tip dips quietly into the water.

After a while, they stop at a grassy patch under a palm tree, above the bank of the canal. They see an ice cream truck. Mary says that she shouldn't really have any because of her diet, but she will because today is such a hot day. She asks Michael and Julia what they want. Julia tells Mary that she has her own money. Michael stays with Jason while Mary and Julia go over to the truck.

A white woman wearing a muumuu smiles and stops by. "Oh, what a beautiful baby. Is he your brother?" Michael tells her no, and she coos at Jason a little more and then continues down the canal. Mary and Julia return with ice cream and a Popsicle for Michael.

"What did that woman want?" Julia asks.

"She was talking to Jason," Michael says. He peels the wrapper off the Popsicle. It is cold and red and sticks to his tongue. Julia has a cup of vanilla ice cream and eats it with a small wooden spoon. Mary has the same and she feeds Jason small white chunks.

"The woman asked me if Jason and I were brothers," Michael says.

"Isn't that stupid," Julia says. "You're Chinese."

"Oh, anything's possible in Hawaii," Mary says and eats a chunk of the ice cream herself. Jason laughs and smiles and slaps Mary's arm, demanding another bite.

"How old are you two?" Mary asks.

"I'm nine." Michael crosses his legs. "Julia is almost thirteen."

"Soon you'll be going to junior high," Mary says to Julia. "How are the schools here?" Mary gives the last bite of her ice cream to Jason, sets the cup on the ground, and pushes the napkin and the spoon into it. Jason claps his hands and screams. "So the schools here are okay, you think?"

"They're fine," Michael says. "They're not too hard."

Jason screams. "Okay, okay," Mary says and picks out the spoon from the cup and hands it to him. "And how is it for you, Julia? How are the boys in school?"

The light falling through the palm leaves above creates crazy patterns on the grass and on Julia's skinny legs. "Oh, they're not so great. Michael goes to my school," Julia laughs.

"You know," Mary says, "the boys." Jason gnaws at the wooden spoon. "Do you like any of the boys in your school?"

Julia's face begins to turn red in the crisscrossed sunshine. "No," she says.

"You will," Mary says. "I remember the boys from my school. I was in love with a different one every week."

"Oh." Julia begins to move around on the grass. She pulls down her shorts to cover her legs. Her T-shirt sticks to her body under her arms with small patches of sweat.

"What about Randy Domingo?" Mary says. "He's a nice-looking boy."

Julia's mouth hangs open and still.

"But you do like him," Michael says, wiping the red Popsicle juice from his lips with the back of his hand.

"*You* like him," she says to Michael.

Jason throws the spoon in the air, and it tumbles near the bank of the canal. Michael opens his crossed legs, and his foot kicks Mary's ice cream cup and napkin down the sloping bank into the water. It floats, bobs up and down, and then sinks.

"Go get it," Julia says. "Litterbug."

After walking a little farther down the canal, they cross the street away from the water and the sunlight and walk back toward home under the shade of the apartment buildings.

In the middle of the row of apartment buildings, they stop in front of a house. "I thought I saw this place from the other side of the street," Mary says. It is an old white house, squat and sandwiched between the buildings. But it is more than a home, according to a sign above its porch. It is also a plant store. Potted plants, big and small, green and yellow, surround the house. Mary carries Jason while Michael pushes the stroller carefully down the front walkway between the plants to the front steps of the porch. An old Japanese woman wearing a straw hat steps out from the front door. The skin around her eyes are crinkly. She smiles. "Hi, hi. How can I help you today?" She holds a shovel.

"I love your plants," Mary says, "the way you let them grow free and wild in your yard. It's like a little paradise. How long have you lived here?"

"A long, long time," says the old woman, shaking her head. "Just after the war, before all of these apartment buildings. When the road along the canal was still unpaved."

They all look around the front yard. "What kind of plants do you like?" the old woman asks Mary.

"Oh, I don't know," Mary says. "Maybe a small plant with flowers, something for my lanai that can take a lot of sun. Unfortunately, nothing too expensive."

"Well, the orchids in back are really the only blooming flowers I have right now, but they don't like too much sun. Besides, they're all pretty expensive." The old women looks around her front yard as if she were a customer.

Inside, the phone rings, and the old woman looks back. It rings again. "Excuse me." She goes into the house.

They leave the stroller near the front porch and walk on a

narrow stone walkway around the side of the house to the back.

"I love the way she lets them all grow wild," Mary says again, leading the way. "They all seem alive and happy."

The orchid house, constructed out of green planks generously spaced to allow sunshine and air in, sits silently under the cool shade of a tall tree. "Oh, I wish I could have an orchid," Mary says, walking up to the green plank house, Jason in her arms. They peer in. Earlike shapes of colors that are not quite colors, pinks brighter than pink, dark whites, and yellows like sunshine sprout from stiff, flaky branches. "Go on in," Mary tells him. She is afraid that Jason will touch the flowers. Julia is not even looking; tired and bored, she walks away. "Go ahead." Mary nods to the door of the greenhouse.

Michael walks in. The floor is covered with tiny white stones. The narrow path between the two tables of plants is large enough for just one person. Michael steps further in. The larger flowers shoot upward; the smaller ones rain down in clusters. Michael waits for them to make a sound. In their clay pots, tightly twined twigs hold down their veiny, hard roots, so much like scary fingers.

"How is it in there?" Mary asks from the other side. She holds Jason close. Her face glows red and white, not quite pink. Mary holds up Jason's hand and waves it at Michael.

"They're beautiful," Michael says so softly that he knows that only Mary can hear him. "They're beautiful." Michael feels the slivers of sunlight falling upon him, the same light that warms the orchids.

Later, in the front yard, the old Japanese woman leads them to a group of plants with dark green leaves, almost like shrubs. "These are gardenias," she says. "I know they're not much to look at now. But they're hearty plants, love lots of light, and if you keep them moist and fertilize them a little, they'll bloom in six months, no more than a year."

Mary holds Jason tightly as she squats beside the plants and turns one of the pots around. The old lady and Michael stand over her. Julia wanders away, bored again. Mary holds her balance with her free hand and pushes herself back up.

"I'll take this one." Mary points with her foot.

Michael bends over near Mary's feet and touches another pot. He reaches into his pocket and hands over the four dollars, store money his mother left for him and Julia, to the old woman. He thinks his mother likes gardenias. He puts his plant in the basket behind Jason's seat, and they continue home. "I don't believe you bought that," Julia says to Michael. Mary holds her plant in her arms, close to her.

As they walk into the front yard of their apartment building, Marie walks down the steps, already dressed in her work uniform.

"I was looking for you two," she says to Michael and Julia. "It's time for dinner." She is smiling hard at Mary. "I hope they were not too much of a bother."

"Oh, no," Mary says. "I love the company."

"Thank you," Marie says, already walking toward home. Mary first carries Jason up the stairs, leaving behind the stroller and the plant near the steps. Michael walks home behind his mother and Julia, holding the gardenia plant.

"Why did you buy that?" Marie asks him as they walk into the kitchen. The table is already set with bowls of rice. Wei stands over the kitchen stove. The meat sizzles in the oil of the wok. Smoke rises.

"It's for you," Michael says. "It's a gardenia plant."

"Oh, that will never bloom," she says. She tells him to put

it out back and wash his hands good before coming to dinner. Marie eats in a hurry and then goes to the bathroom to put on her makeup. Julia and Michael stare at the dark green spinach leaves in their bowls of soup. Marie walks by them again, says goodbye, and heads out the door, back to the restaurant.

THEY SIT out on Mary's lanai, the sun over them; Mary lies on her chaise longue wearing big, dark sunglasses, her hair tied up in a ponytail, her face red and perspiring. She tells them about her new diet, which she found in a magazine, that allows her a thousand calories a day. She can no longer have teriyaki hamburgers or ice cream. Mary says that she is glad that she lives in Hawaii because of all the fresh fruit here. Mary is bigger than their mother. Their father is much smaller than Bob.

"Have you lost any weight?" Michael asks Mary.

The hot sun pounds on his head. The tips of a few of the leaves of Mary's gardenia plant have turned brown. Michael wants to tell Mary that it will never bloom.

"Oh, a little," she answers his question. "I think this new diet is it this time. I don't mind eating the food it tells me to. But I do have to be careful about getting all my vitamins and enough protein." She tells them that she measures out her food by the cup and adds up her calories at the end of each day.

"So how much weight have you lost?" Michael asks.

Julia begins to giggle. She is fanning herself with a magazine. "Boy, it's hot," she says.

Mary does not answer Michael's question. Beads of sweat form on her forehead. Her face is red. Michael wonders if she didn't hear him. Her eyes are behind dark glasses, in perfect circles, and Michael can't tell if they are open or shut.

"How do we know that you lost any weight?" Michael says to Mary. "Prove it to us."

"I don't have to prove anything to you," she says as she sits up and rips the glasses off her face and points the tip of one earpiece at him. "I don't have to prove anything to you. If you don't like it, you can leave." She stops talking but keeps looking at Michael for another moment, her eyes squinting out the sunlight. Michael sweats through his T-shirt. He can feel Julia sitting next to him but no longer hears the flapping of the magazine.

Michael doesn't get up when Mary tells him that he can leave if he doesn't like it. He doesn't want to go. He doesn't know anywhere else he'd rather be at the moment. After a while Mary lies back again, puts her sunglasses back on, and looks out at the sky. Michael can feel the breeze of Julia's magazine again. Sweat shines on Mary's white neck, and Michael feels it on his own.

Soon they hear their father calling them to dinner, his voice rising to the lanai. Mary says goodbye, not getting up from her seat, telling them that she should be getting Bob's dinner ready soon, too.

As they walk down the stairs, Michael wonders if they were bothering Mary.

ONE MORNING Michael wakes up alone, climbs to the top of the stairs, and silently watches from behind the grate of the railing as Mary, Jason, and Bob drive out of the parking lot. They look like they're going to the beach. Both Jason and Bob are shirtless.

Julia is still sleeping. Michael feels lonely by himself.

The morning goes on forever. After a while, Julia comes up the stairs and stands by Michael, looking down at the empty parking lot. She doesn't say anything. Michael begins to get hungry but is too afraid to ask her if she wants to go home to make lunch. Randy's car drives down the street, the surfboard sticking out of the back-seat window. Randy parks and gets out of the car, his skin darker than before. He sees Michael and Julia looking at him. Leaving the surfboard in the car, he walks toward the corner store.

Suddenly Julia grabs Michael's hand, and together they run down the stairs out into the parking lot. Michael feels excited; heat rises off the concrete, and he begins to sweat. Julia pulls him in the direction of the corner store. He doesn't try to pull away because he's happy she came out to play. Her grasp is tight and moist.

They follow Randy through the air-conditioned store. Randy stands over the ice cream freezer, his head bent down to the glass, deciding what he wants. Michael and Julia hide behind a shelf of spices. When Randy walks toward the register, they go to the ice cream freezer. They stick their heads in and take deep breaths of the cold air and blow out smoke. It dries up the inside of their noses. They touch all the ice cream bars and finally decide on a red Popsicle to share between them. As Randy leaves the store they go up to the register and pay, and Julia breaks the Popsicle into two sticks against the edge of the counter. Outside the store the Popsicle sticks instantly begin to perspire. Michael looks down the street and sees Randy far ahead of them.

They hold hands, and their running turns to skipping as they near Randy. They lick their red sticks out loud between each step. They all enter the parking lot at the same time. Michael and Julia giggle like babies. Randy turns toward them. He is eating an ice cream sandwich. His dark back sweats down the middle. Julia laughs louder. They can almost touch Randy.

Julia kicks out her foot. She pretends to kick at Randy's sandals as he picks them up with each step. Julia sings laughter into her red microphone. She lets go of Michael and steps closer to Randy. Michael runs up and grabs her wrist this time and pulls her up behind Randy as she kicks out at him again. She knocks Randy's sandal off his foot, and his ice cream sandwich falls to the ground. He stops abruptly. Julia backs away, bracing herself against the side of his car. Michael falls forward against Randy, his red stick stabbing Randy's back. He grabs Randy's legs as he falls to the ground. Randy steps away from him.

"Leave me alone," he says, going over to his sandal. He reaches back to touch the wet, sticky spot on his back. "Go away, you two," he says. "Dumbheads."

"You leave *us* alone," Julia says, standing up from his car, her hands on her waist. "You leave us alone."

Randy pulls his surfboard from the back seat of his car and goes inside the apartment building.

Michael's Popsicle, broken into small pieces and covered with dirt, melts on the pavement. His knee begins to hurt and then begins to bleed. He watches Randy as he walks by the railing above.

Julia turns toward Michael. "Why did you make me run into him? Why?" She walks away from him, back inside.

At the bathroom sink Michael drips warm water on his knee. It runs down his leg to the floor. Julia comes in and makes him sit down on the toilet. From the medicine cabinet she takes out a plastic bottle of Bactine and a cotton ball and rubs the cold, sweet-smelling liquid on his knee, slowly wiping away the blood and dirt. His knee jerks up and down as his sobbing turns to heavy breathing.

That night Michael goes to bed early, before his mother comes home. A little while later he hears Julia come in. Julia has draped a sheet over the opening of her bunk, like an enclosed tent, her own private bedroom. The extra bed, once adjacent to the bunk bed, is now gone. Michael must now climb up and down a wooden ladder, squeaking and shaking with his weight, to get to his bunk. Julia lies still below him. His hand lingers along the steel frame. He imagines that Julia is thinking about Randy. His hand dangles over the side of the bed as his eyes close.

The bed shakes. He pulls his hand up. He looks over the railing. The bed shifts suddenly. He holds on to the mattress, waiting to fall down upon Julia.

ROBBED

THEY COME home late from a kung fu movie. Their apartment has been robbed. Light escapes from the cracked doorway. Marie, with Julia in her arms, pushes open the door. The apartment is a mess. *"Dil*—fuck," Marie says.

Wei disappears into the bedroom. In the kitchen Marie calls the police. Julia sits on the kitchen counter. She imagines the burglar hiding in the bedroom closet, ready to attack her father. The kitchen is neat and clean. The burglar must not have been hungry. Julia picks out a sesame biscuit from the glass jar on the counter and munches on it. Her father does not scream from the bedroom.

Marie sets Julia on the floor and they go into the living room. They pick up books and magazines from the floor and stack them on the black vinyl sofa. An orchid plant, originally on the windowsill, lies on the carpet. The window is broken, and one of the three flowering branches of the plant is bent. Pieces of glass litter the carpet. The flowers are purple ears. They do not smell fragrant; they smell of nothing. Marie picks up the plant and sets it back on the sill. It looks sick. She picks up Julia and they both look out the broken window. The burglar must have climbed up the mango tree onto the ledge, entered through the window, and then escaped through the front door. Marie picks out pieces of glass from the plant's pot. She cuts her thumb but does not cry.

Wei calls for Marie from the bedroom. While holding Julia in one arm, Marie walks and sucks on her bleeding thumb. The bedroom is the messiest room. The dresser drawers hang open, and the clothes are scattered about. Wei points to the closet. Marie's dresses lie dead and stained red on the floor. "The burglar must've cut his hand on the glass when he came in through the window," Wei explains.

"Damn it." Marie stares at her bleeding thumb. "All of this has to be washed tomorrow before I go to the hospital," she mumbles with the thumb in her mouth. She sets Julia on the bed and reaches for a tissue from the box on the dresser and wraps it around the thumb.

Back in the kitchen, Marie sets Julia back on the counter and takes a white take-out box from the refrigerator. She flips open the flaps of the box with one hand, turns the cold noodles onto a plate, and eats with chopsticks. "I can't believe I'm hungry again. I guess the baby wants to eat as much as she can before she's aborted." Wei fills a drinking glass with water in which he puts the orchid branch. Marie picks up strands of yellow noodles. The tissue around the finger on the injured hand is red.

Marie sets down the chopsticks and goes to the bathroom for a bandage. Wei picks up the plate of noodles and begins to eat.

IN THE morning, downstairs in the back laundry room, Marie washes several loads of red-spotted clothes.

On the living-room sofa, Julia sits amid the freshly dried laundry. It's warm and smells clean. Wei measures the broken window, jotting down numbers on a pad. He takes off the frame, replacing it with a large piece of cardboard stuck on with strips of masking tape. "Watch it," Wei tells Julia. "Make sure no one comes in while I get the glass fixed."

Julia watches the cardboard window as Marie comes in and drops more laundry on the sofa. "Where'd your father go?" she asks. "I've got to be at the hospital before twelve." She picks out a few items from the sofa and stuffs them into a blue Pan Am bag. She goes to the bathroom and returns with her toothbrush, a plastic comb, and a can of hair spray. She puts them into the bag with the warm clothes.

Wei comes home with a new window and puts it in. They drive to the hospital and drop Marie at the entrance. "I'll call you," she says as she walks away. Wei drives home with Julia. He lies on the sofa with Julia, playing with her ball-shaped radio, at his feet. The burglar took the TV. Wei stares out the window and falls asleep.

The phone rings and Wei goes over to answer it. After several okays and yeses, he hangs up and returns to the sofa. "They'll operate in an hour. We'll go back to the hospital later on."

He goes to the kitchen and pulls out a couple sheets of

white paper and a black marker from the drawer. He writes: NOTHING INSIDE.

In the living room, he sets the sheet on the new glass of the window and tapes it on. The ink is dark and seeps through the paper. He sets the roll of tape next to the orchid plant. "I'm tired," he says. "I have to lie down. Do you want to watch TV?" The TV is gone. He goes to the bedroom. Julia, alone, stares at her father's sign. It reads: E D I S N I   G N I H T O N.

IN THE hospital waiting room she holds the pot of the orchid plant between her legs while sitting on the large orange vinyl sofa. "That's such a pretty plant," says an old woman sitting beside Julia. "I have orchid plants at home. But mine are in bigger pots and have hundreds of flowers." The old woman wears a muumuu and holds a Chinese newspaper. "Where are your parents?" she asks Julia. Julia points down the corridor where Wei disappeared. "Do you speak Chinese?" the old woman asks. Julia nods. "Never forget your Chinese. My kids are grown and can't speak a word of it. They understand what I say to them, but they can't answer me back in Chinese. What a shame. They speak English to me. I'm too old to learn English." She unfolds her newspaper and holds it up. Her eyes are red. One of her front teeth is gold, and she hunches over a little to read the characters on the paper. A candy bar sits inside the pot of the orchid plant. Wei purchased it from a vending machine before abandoning Julia to look for the doctor. The roots of the orchid are thick, tangled like varicose veins, and cling to the twigs in the pot. Some roots grow out of the clay pot and run down along its sides. The old woman tilts her head back and closes her eyes.

She sits still, breathing audibly. She then hums a Chinese folk tune, which Julia immediately recognizes as one her mother plays on the tape machine. She moves the orchid from between her legs to the empty seat beside her. She picks out the candy bar and unwraps it. The old woman opens her eyes at the sound of the wrapper crinkling and stares down at Julia. Julia offers the old woman a bite. "No, thank you," she says. "I don't have any more teeth to eat candy. My kids eat too much American junk food. They don't eat the Chinese food I cook for them."

When Wei returns to the waiting room he says to Julia, "Let's go see Mom."

The old woman mumbles and smiles at Wei. "Good girl," she says, meaning Julia.

Marie's room is small and white. The fluorescent light overhead makes the room glow ghostly. The bed is a maze of steel bars graced with perfect white sheets. A thin tube in Marie's right arm runs up to a sack of clear liquid. She is silent and still, with her eyes closed. Wei walks up to her. He does not touch her or the bed. He stares for a long moment, places the orchid plant on the side table next to the phone, and then turns and walks to the glass window. He looks out. Julia climbs into the only chair in the room, a big yellow chair with wooden arms. She wonders if her mother is ignoring her and just pretending to sleep. It's too early to sleep. From the chair Julia sees what her father sees outside. There is no ledge outside the window.

A doctor comes in. He is taller than Wei. His hair is thick and black, combed to one side. He wears black-framed glasses and holds a wooden clipboard. Wei turns toward him. Marie opens her eyes. "How are you doing?" he asks Marie.

"Just okay," she mumbles.

"You should feel much better in the morning. Next time don't wait so long or you'll just have to have the baby."

"Okay, Doctor," Marie answers him.

"There's nothing to worry about?" Wei asks.

"No. I'll be back in the morning to check you out, Marie. Goodnight."

Marie speaks up, "Doctor, do you like plants? Didn't you tell me you have a small flower garden?"

"Yes," he answers her.

"Why don't you take this orchid plant home and add it to your garden? They brought it for me, but since I'll be leaving in the morning, I'll have no use for it here."

The doctor walks over to the plant. He picks it up. "It's beautiful," he says. "I have a few small orchids. None of them have bloomed yet. My wife loves orchids. Thank you." He takes the plant and walks to the door. "Sleep now. You'll feel much better in the morning."

"Thank you, Doctor," Marie says and closes her eyes again.

Wei turns around and stares out the window again.

Marie starts up, "That was no fun." She speaks as if she were out of breath.

"You know we could not have afforded another girl."

"Well, you better go to the temple and pray harder next time for a boy. I'm not doing this again," she states. "I'm tired and want to sleep."

"Okay." Wei reaches over for Julia's hand and helps her off the chair. "We'll come back for you in the morning."

"Yeah, okay." Her eyes close again. "Turn the light off."

As Wei and Julia walk out, Julia looks back quickly in the dark room to see an even darker sky beyond the window.

AT HOME Julia sleeps on the living-room sofa with a blanket and her ball-shaped radio playing low. Wei bought take-out from the local chop suey house, sweet-and-sour pork and shrimp fried rice, and father and daughter ate silently at the kitchen table graced by the purple orchids. Wei tells Julia to go to sleep early; they will pick up Mommy tomorrow. He goes into the bedroom and shuts the door, and light escapes from below the closed door. Julia lies still, looking out the living-room window. Her father's sign glows in the streetlight. The leaves of the mango tree outside cast funny patterns on the ceiling. Shapes of light and dark dance when the wind blows.

Julia imagines a burglar breaking the window with his hand. The white sign rips in half. Pieces of glass fall noiselessly to the carpeted floor. The burglar comes in, looks around, and sees nothing inside. An empty room except for her, sleeping on the sofa. He picks her up, wrapped in the blanket, and rocks her in his arms. He walks over to the window and climbs out. He hoists her on his back. She holds tight. He climbs down the mango tree and takes her away.

OPEN HOUSE

ONE EVENING, driving home from mah-jongg at Auntie Vickie and Uncle Mo's, Michael concluded that people only want what they don't have.

Earlier, Auntie Vickie informed Marie and Wei that she and Uncle Mo were planning to buy a new house in the suburbs for an investment. When Auntie Vickie and Julia went to the kitchen for the refreshments, Marie whispered to Wei, "I want a house in the suburbs."

"So do I," Wei said. "But we have Michael and Julia instead. They are our investments. Now if we didn't have them, of course, we would have more money."

Sometimes Michael wished that Uncle Mo were his father. At the table, he and Uncle Mo continued to stack the mah-jongg tiles on top of each other.

"Let's see how high we can build this tower," Uncle Mo proposed.

"What if it falls?" Michael asked, giggling.

At that moment, Auntie Vickie, with a trayful of cups of hot tea, and Julia, with a tray of candied vegetables and fruits, returned to the living room.

"Marie, Wei, let's play," Auntie Vickie said. "Mo, stop fooling around."

Michael sadly watched Uncle Mo take apart the mah-jongg tower. Michael remembered Uncle Mo telling him once that he wished that Michael were his son, how he wanted a son . . . .

I WANT to have a baby because I'm already thirty-five and it's time for us to start our family. If we wait any longer, I won't have a son grown up in time to take care of me when I am old. I calculate if we have him soon, when I turn sixty-one, the begin-ning of my golden years, my son will have graduated from American schools and have a high-paying job.

"A baby costs money," Vickie tells me. "It doesn't make sense to have one right now. Let's wait. *I* have plenty of time. Let's save some money first. We are in America now. We have to be careful what we do. If something goes wrong, everything will go wrong. Then we won't even be able to afford the boat ride back to Hong Kong."

And then my ever-pragmatic wife tells me what I think is the true reason she doesn't want to have a baby: she wants to wait until her career is *off its feet*, like an American woman does. My wife sells jewelry restaurant-to-restaurant, jade bracelets and pendants, gold chains, all imported from Hong Kong, which she gets from her Taiwanese boss, a tall dark skinny *gwei lou*—Mr. Devil—who chain-smokes. She met him originally at the chop suey house where she used to work when we first arrived in Honolulu. That's what they call small Chinese restaurants here. Chop suey is not Chinese; it's what Americans think Chinese food is: all chopped and mixed up.

My wife told me that her boss told her: "With a face like yours, soft like ivory, I would buy anything from you." *Gwei lou.* She tells me he told her that she's his best salesman. I can see how she's a good salesman: she's pushy and sexy and knows how to talk. Her boss wants to make her his partner someday. Open a jewelry shop together. Fifty-fifty. I don't like him giving her his jewelry so freely; it makes them too close. They shouldn't trust each other: she's Chinese and he's Taiwanese.

But I think ever since she started selling her jade the greedy green of it has been sinking into her skin. This is her latest scheme: there's a suburb going up just outside of Honolulu and the houses are cheap. She gets the idea from her boss to buy one, and then to rent it out to other people. That's an *investment,* she tells me. Meanwhile, we continue to live in our small apartment with no son. Her boss told her that he would help her with the down payment: now he's offering her money. If she successfully rents out the house immediately after buying it, then we won't lose a cent. In a couple of years she can sell at a *profit,* the only reward of an *investment.* I don't understand how you can buy a house and not live in it yourself.

In the morning my wife tells me what to wear to the realtor's. She tells me we have to be careful when we talk to him, since our English is poor. She doesn't want to be cheated because she can't understand some technical American term. I remind her it is her idea to buy a house we don't plan to live in.

"We can't live there," she tells me again, as she starts the car. "It's too far. I need to be near my customers."

"We have a car."

My wife looks sternly at me with pressed red lips.

I know how to annoy her further. "In China I used to walk five miles every morning just to go to school." I think it was only two.

"We're not in China anymore."

You see, it was her big idea to come to Hawaii, *Tan Hong San.* Others were going to Hawaii. It sounded like paradise. But there are tall buildings and cars here, too. Hong Kong was at least all Chinese. Here there are all kinds of people and they come to the fish market where I work and try to talk to me in English, and all I can do is nod and point and wrap up their orders. At six in the morning when I unload the crates from the trunk, the fishes are still moving. I wash and scale them under cold water. I wear Playtex rubber gloves so the cold won't hurt my hands. By seven-thirty I have all the fishes, dead and still now, displayed on a bed of crushed ice behind the glass under the fluorescent bulb. Kumu, a local Pacific fish, is our best seller. It has a red body and its meat is white, thick like chicken's. I like to steam it with a little soy sauce, oil, crushed ginger, and chopped scallions.

My wife times the drive to the suburb, looking at her watch every few minutes. She insists quietly, "There's really no way we can live this far away from the city. You would have to get up before you go to bed just to make it to market on time. And how you hate going there! And you have such problems sleeping as is." She shakes her head.

You wonder why I can't sleep, I think to her. Could you, if you had to sleep next to you every night?

"This will be a good *investment*," she says in the same breath. "My boss said that he would buy one for himself if he didn't already have so many other *investments.*"

WE HAVE just enough time before our appointment with the re-altor to take a tour of the six model homes. Other families roam in and out of the houses: I guess that's why it's called *open house.* Five of the six yards are arranged with trees, bushes, and smooth green lawns. The sixth yard is in the style of a Japanese garden, little white rocks all around, on one side a miniature pagoda and on the other side a *bonsai* tree, crooked and pokey. "They must have hired professional decorators," my wife surmises.

We go into a house. The curtains match the wallpaper, and the wallpaper matches the carpet. A chandelier hangs over a dining-room table surrounded by eight chairs. "Who needs eight chairs?" my wife asks anyone who's around. *We* never have anyone over for dinner. I do all the cooking. My wife would say she is too tired to cook after selling all day, but the truth is she can't even boil rice without burning it. "More water, more water," I tell her. Beyond the screen door of the model home's living room is a concrete patio complete with green lawn furni-ture and a modern stand-up grill. Sometimes my wife and I take a break from Chinese food, and I grill a T-bone outside the front door of our apartment. I pour a little whiskey and soy sauce over it while it cooks. Smoke stings my eyes. I chop the steak into bite-size pieces and serve it up to my wife with a small plate of ketchup. She's made the side dishes: mashed potatoes from a box and a chopped-up tomato smeared with mayonnaise and sprinkled black with pepper.

I make the other people in the model home disappear in

my mind. This is my house, my dining room, my patio. My wife and I have outdoor parties. We invite the neighbors, grill hamburgers and hot dogs, and serve Primo beer, with Jell-O for dessert.

THE REALTOR, a Japanese man, wears an aloha shirt showing off dark, wrinkled arms (too much golf). He smiles white teeth at my wife when he tells us to sit. I notice my wife wearing extra jewelry. She wears her prized jade bracelet, the one with the gold hinge and clasp. She doesn't like forcing conventional jade bracelets over her hand. And besides, she's not the kind of Chinese woman who wears her bracelet at all times; she slips it on when she likes, and always takes it off before going to bed. The top button of her silky blouse is undone: two gold chains lay against her white chest. A tiny Buddha hangs on to one and drops out of her cleavage when she leans close to the realtor over his desk to hear what he is saying.

I can understand only every other word he is saying, and I strain my eyes to listen closer. My wife's English is better than mine; she took an evening class at a local high school within the first month of our arriving in Honolulu. I look penitently at her to tell me what the realtor is saying, and in spurts during the pauses in his speech, she tells me in Chinese: "They're one hundred thousand dollars apiece—more for added accessories, like a dishwasher or central air (we don't need those things) . . . ten percent down . . . low interest . . . we have to fill out an application and take it to the bank . . . they don't like foreigners, like those Japanese coming over and buying up the island . . . they don't allow—" My wife stops suddenly. I quickly turn to the realtor and I see his lips say the word *investment*. My wife is silent.

and have lunch at a hotel's restaurant. Just trees, beaches, the ocean—what I thought Hawaii was like before I arrived here.

But this Saturday my wife goes to Chinatown to sell her jewelry, leaving me at home alone, telling me she's only thinking about the house. I don't say anything as she leaves; I want to say, I don't want to buy a house we're not going to live in. You just don't want to go to the other side of the island with me. It always has to be your way.

After she leaves, I go across the street to the chop suey house for lunch. The place is empty except for a couple of Hawaiian construction men, fat and dark, eating bowls of wonton noodle soup and drinking Primo. I sit near the kitchen door and wait for the waitress. Taped on the walls are pink strips of paper announcing today's specials; beside them are pictures, cut out from old calendars, of famous places in China I've never been to before. My favorite is the picture of the Summer Palace to where the Dowager Empress escaped during the revolutionary uprisings. The palace looks like it's floating in the water. The empress was an evil and demanding woman.

The waitress's face appears in the window of the kitchen door. She sees me and comes out. She's not like the waitresses who buy my wife's jewelry; this one looks like she's fresh off the boat. She smiles; her face is clean of makeup. She hands me a menu and then turns back to the kitchen. Knotted around her soft, skinny white neck are the straps of her apron; below, her sharp shoulder blades shift beneath the thin cloth of her blouse as she pushes the door. Running water, chopping knives, clanking steel woks—all these noises escape through the closing crack.

The Hawaiian men wobble out. I am alone.

I get up and go over to the kitchen door and look in its square window. Her small white fingers spread out wide over the thick wooden handle of the wok to hold it balanced as she picks it up. She looks at the flame underneath and turns it up to orange-and-blue, sets down the wok, and then drops a spatulaful of oil into the warming steel bowl. Holding the handle, she moves the wok back and forth: oil slides and dribbles across the black surface. She reaches back for a handful of red, raw pieces of meat and tosses them into the center. Wiping her hand on the apron, she steps back as the meat sizzles. Smoke hits the ceiling. She picks up the wok again, scrapes the meat up with the steel spatula, flipping it over, raw side down. In succession, she adds the vegetables—baby corn, broccoli pieces, carrot slices; sauces shot vigorously from squirt bottles; a little more oil to loosen it up, all the time shaking the wok, bringing it up and down, away and toward the fire. Lifting the wok again effortlessly, she tilts it and with the spatula pushes the hot food into the open mouth of the waiting white take-out box. It all slides in. She sets the wok down and turns off the flame. I pull away from the window.

I sit down, pick up the menu, and pretend to read.

The waitress emerges with the white box in hand. "Know what you want?" she calls to me from the counter, as she bags the box. She walks toward me. Her apron is stained with raw beef.

"I'm hungry," I say. "How about a kumu?"

"Oh, I'm sorry, but we don't have such a big fish in the kitchen."

"I work at the fish market," I tell her.

"Oh, yeah," she says, "then why don't you bring one in and I'll fix it up for you."

SIX WEEKS go by and the loan comes through for the house. My wife gets her investment. The night before we plan to go to the bank to sign the papers, we sit at the kitchen table under the fluorescent light, counting up the money we have for the down payment: our checking and saving accounts plus the check from my wife's boss. I punch the figures into the calculator as my wife reads them off. I tell her that we are still short a couple thousand dollars. For a moment I can't believe she can make that kind of mistake, miscount, but then I see her smiling maniacally, her eyes twinkling. She goes over to the sink, reaches under it, and pulls out a tin coffee can. Opening it up, she pulls out a bundle of bills. "This is what I've been doing all these past Saturdays," she tells me, waving the green bills. Twenties, tens, hundreds. "Another hundred," she calls out, and I punch in the number. So much money from selling jade. "Another, another!" After a while she stops. "How much?" she demands. I read out the figure: we are still short. "That's impossible!" she says and rips the calculator out of my hand. I'm glad we don't have enough money. All those Saturdays spent for nothing. I laugh. "What are you laughing for?" "I guess I don't want this house as much as you do." "Do you have a better plan how not to be poor for the rest of our lives? I guess you're content to work at the fish market forever. Well, not me. I'm not going to be a salesman forever. Now let's count it all again," she says. "I know there is enough money here. We'll stay up all night if we have to."

The following day my wife's boss gives her another check for eight hundred dollars.

AFTER WE get the house, she does what her boss tells her and puts an ad in the newspaper. People call and she talks to them in her broken English: *"Three bedroom. Two bathrooms. All new. Very clean. Very nice."* We rent the house to a white military couple with a baby boy. The wife is short, her hair yellow, her arms fleshy. Her husband's hair is cut to the scalp. The military base is not far from the suburb.

A WEEK before the family moves in, my wife asks me if I want to spend a night at the house. "Sleep there," she adds.

I look at her and wonder what she's plotting.

"We can bring blankets, food." Then she tells me the reason: if the realtor ever finds out about the rental, we could always tell him that we tried to live in the house but couldn't because the commute was too much and we therefore had to rent it out to pay the mortgage.

She thinks of everything.

FRIDAY AFTER work we drive out to the suburb. In the back seat are sheets, blankets, pillows, paper plates, paper towels, forks, knives, the hibachi, charcoal, and a bag of food: a T-bone, store-bought potato salad, a tomato, orange juice, mayonnaise, and ketchup.

The front yard is all dirt. The military wife told us she wants to make the yard beautiful with grass, trees, and flowers. "I know she'll just let weeds grow all over," my wife says exasperatedly.

At the door, we take off our shoes. She turns on all the lights. The walls are shiny white and the carpet smells new and clean. The house seems bigger without furniture. My wife goes to the kitchen and sets her briefcase on the counter. She was afraid of leaving it at home alone overnight.

In the bedroom, she makes up our temporary bed, laying the sheet on the carpet, placing the pillows where the head of the bed would be if there were a bed, and then covering it all up with a blanket. "It's cooler out here in the country," she comments. "It's good we brought along an extra blanket."

On the patio, I start up the hibachi. I fan the smoke from the coals with a folded paper bag.

We sit outside on the patio floor, afraid of spilling anything on the carpet. "I know these white people are going to mess up the house, so no use getting too attached to it. They won't care," she says, "because they don't own it. Now if I lived here I would buy all new furniture, plant flowers, maybe even a mango tree in the backyard. It's a beautiful house. It's too bad we can't live here."

I remain quiet as I eat my steak. I don't like her talking like it's our house.

SHE SLEEPS soundly beside me, flat on her back, her arms crossed over herself. I feel the carpet poking me through the sheet and this keeps me up. I open my eyes, and the room is as black as when they were closed. We are in the country. Getting up off the floor, I go to the living room and begin to imagine furniture everywhere around: we live here, I say to myself. It doesn't work and I feel relieved. I don't want to live in this house anymore. Alone here with my wife. It's just that I don't think I like her as

I used to. She doesn't need me: she knows how to make her own money, how to buy a house. Whereas the waitress at the chop suey house would need me, not knowing Honolulu and English as well as she wants to, as she told me once. I know how she feels. I know how it feels to be afraid and uncomfortable in a foreign place.

I go down the hallway to one of the empty bedrooms. The streetlights do not come in like they do back at the apartment. There, when I could not fall asleep, I would go out into the living room and look out its window at the chop suey house down below. The paper sign on the door told me it was closed, but the interior lights indicated that she was still there. I waited at my window. In the alleyway, the waitress braced open the kitchen door of the restaurant with her foot as she pulled with both hands at a large trash can filled with the discarded food of the day, to be picked up later on, sometime in the early morning, by the man from the pig farm. That was what she told me, when she told me how much she disliked her job. The tips were never good. But she didn't have anywhere else to go. She didn't know enough English to work in a nicer Chinese restaurant. The trash can scraped painfully on the ground, and it took her a while to position it in the right spot. She made sure the lid was secure in its place, fearful of alley cats getting in. Her face turned upward toward the streetlight that stood just outside my window; I pulled back from the light. She wiped her hands on her apron and reached back to free the pins from her hair. Long and black it fell, and the wind lifted, washing away the smells of the restaurant. She closed her eyes on the light, the make-believe moon. But before her face dared to show any more emotion, she turned back into the alleyway. I stepped up to the window again. The kitchen door slammed shut. I looked hard at the streetlight, closed my eyes, and turned back into the living room. I could still see the light in front of my eyes, strong and bright for a moment before it faded away as I returned to my sleeping wife.

In the new house, I return to the bedroom and lie back down on the floor beside her. Sometimes I can lie awake for hours. "Oh, I can't sleep," I moan to wake her up. She crawls on top of me, holds me, and strokes my hair, all the time looking in my eyes and asking me what is the matter. Her eyes are black and calm. She sits up and wiggles off the straps of her night-gown; it crumples down on me. Moonlight spotlights her ivory breast. My hands run up her sides, and I hold them tightly. My wife does the work when we make love, and I like the way she does it.

THE FOLLOWING morning, after having orange juice, we pack up to leave. As she starts up the car, she looks over at me and smiles. "It's Saturday," she says. "Our day off. We haven't spent a Saturday together in a long time. What would you like to do? Drive to the other side of the island? We're already halfway there." I don't know what's come over her, and I can only nod.

WHEN WE arrive home later that evening, past dinner time, I suggest to my wife that I go get some take-out. But instead she looks at me as if she is still remembering our lovemaking last night, and says, "Why don't we eat at the chop suey house tonight? It's still early. Saves us from washing dishes, and besides, it's nice to be served now and then."

"Are you sure?" I ask her. "It's getting late. I wonder how much longer they'll be open. Take-out is fast. I can run in and out."

"It'll be fine," she says, while backing into the parking space. "Let's eat out."

I rush up to her side as she hurries to the chop suey house, swinging her briefcase as if she is going there to discover something. I slow down a little, wondering if the waitress will start talking to me the way she does when I go there alone. I wonder if she will think my wife is my wife.

We look in. It is completely empty inside. The sign says it's still open, though I see the mop and bucket in the corner. My wife leads me in and to a table beside the window. She sets her briefcase on the floor against the wall.

"Look at the moon's beautiful white face," she says, pointing up past the characters painted on the window. "Last night," she continues, "after you got up, I saw the moonlight coming softly into the room. I got up and looked at it for a while. It seemed so much brighter in the country, with no streetlights competing with it, pretending to be her."

I look at the moon but can only see the streetlights. I turn away from the window, and I see the waitress approaching. She silently sets down menus and a pot of tea.

"It's such a beautiful house," my wife starts up again. "Oh, if it were only just a little nearer, we could have actually thought about living there. All that space and quiet. I bet you could sleep better out there." She reaches across the table and pats my hand. I avoid looking at her by busying myself with preparing a soy sauce-and-mustard mixture in my little dish. "Please pour me a little," she asks. "And a just tiny dab of mustard." I pour the black liquid into her dish.

"My jewelry business is going very well. I've been thinking about your wanting to start a family. Maybe in a couple of years, after we sell the house." I don't say anything. I don't think she knows what she's talking about, but she continues. "Don't you still want a son?" She's smiling. Why is she being so nice? Why is she acting this way? She has her house; I don't need her to make concessions to me.

The waitress emerges from the kitchen. My wife wipes her chopsticks and mine, preparing for the food to arrive. The waitress holds a large plate of noodles in one hand and two smaller plates in the other. She seems no longer to know me. My wife pushes aside the teapot, making room for everything. Slowly the waitress sets down the two plates in front of us and then the plate of steaming hot noodles. It knocks gently against the teapot, nuzzling itself among the crowded table. Then I see my wife's dish of soy sauce tipping. The black liquid slides across the table over the edge and onto her. My wife stands up. The waitress steps back.

"*Dil*—fuck!" my wife screams. "It's all over me."

The waitress reaches for a clean napkin from an adjacent table, hands it to my wife, picks up the tilted dish, and wipes up the spilt sauce with my napkin. "Do you want a towel?"

My wife dabs at the sauce stains on her pants. "What's the use now? My pants are already ruined." She sits down again only after checking the seat for sauce. "It's too late. It's already stained."

The waitress stands a moment longer before returning to the kitchen.

"What are you looking at?" my wife snaps at me. "Why are you looking at her? She's not getting a tip, that's for sure." She scoops large pieces of pork onto her plate. "This stain will never come out. My good pants, no less." She greedily eats her noodles.

We finish the entire plate of food in a matter of minutes. "Let's go. Let's get out of here," she says. "Go. Go and pay."

I stand up, but before I can walk away I feel her slapping my arm.

"Remember not to give her a tip." My wife doesn't take her eyes off me.

The waitress sees me through the kitchen window and comes out. She is smiling meekly, for the first time all evening. We meet at the register. "Everything okay?" she asks me.

I hand her the money. "Yes," I whisper, "it was all very good." She gives me back the change. I hold my hand out, palm down. "No, no," I say softly, so my wife can't hear. Our hands touch and I look at her, but she doesn't look as if she understands what I'm trying to say. She looks exhausted. "Keep it," I say boldly. "Keep it." I withdraw my hand, and her fist clenches the money and forces it into her apron pocket. She now understands my wife is my wife. She goes over to the mop and begins churning up the soapy water in the bucket.

I turn around and my wife is gone. Outside, through the glass, I see her clutching her briefcase as she crosses the street to our apartment. The waitress has already begun to mop the floor, and water slides toward me, pushing me out of the chop suey house. I run out and cross the street, all the time hoping my wife will not be angry at me.

Nervously, I walk into our apartment. She is nowhere in sight. I go to the bedroom. On the bed, she lies flat on her stomach, her face buried in her hands. It sounds as if she is crying, but I'm not sure because I've never seen her cry before. I sit on the edge of the bed, and still she does not move. I don't know if I should touch her. "What's the matter?" I finally ask.

Her face emerges from her palms. Her eyes are moist. It looks as if it took effort on her part to muster up that bit of emotion.

"I'm sorry," I say.

"Sorry for what?" Her face turns to me; a few strands of her black hair are stuck between her red lips.

"For not listening to you. For giving the waitress a tip."

"Is that it?"

I don't know what else she wants me to say.

She tells me, "That's not all. That's not it, and you know it. I saw how she was looking at you: she likes you and you know she does, and still you gave her a tip."

She is jealous.

"I work hard," she continues. "What haven't I done for you? Day after day. Sell, sell, sell. I'm a good wife."

"Of course. Yes." I nod. I feel like crying but don't because if I do, I won't be able to stop for a long time, because she is right, she is a good wife, and I don't deserve her.

CHINESE MOVIE

MOM TAKES Julia and me to Chinatown to see the American movie at the old, smelly Hawaii Theater. The windows of the car are rolled down in the hot afternoon. She asks us to help her find a parking space. My hands hang out the window. "Over there," I tell her.

"No, that's a fire hydrant, Michael."

I see Julia in the rearview mirror sitting in the back with crossed arms. A red sweater lies beside her. "I get to sit in the front on the ride home," she had said earlier when I jumped in the front seat.

"Hurry and find that parking space," Mom repeats. "The movie will start soon."

Julia yells from the back, "I hope it's over by the time we get there."

We drive around the block of the theater for the third time. Near the movie posters, a wrinkled old Chinese man wearing a pair of khaki shorts and an aloha flower-print shirt smokes a cigarette and takes tickets from moviegoers. The poster advertises today's feature, *Beyond the House of Terror*.

We stop at the stoplight beyond the theater, and a tall black lady enters the sidewalk from the red doorway of a bar. She turns to point her middle finger at two white sailors who follow her out. One doesn't wear any shirt, only white pants and a blue striped cap. His chest is hairy, and he has a rose tattoo on his arm. He stands tall, and the shorter one leans on him and holds a beer bottle. The taller sailor shouts at the black lady, "Knock, knock." Her blond beehive hairdo is tilting off her head, and her fishnet stockings are pulled tight over her long legs.

"Who's there?" answers the shorter sailor. He sticks his face in the hairy chest of his friend and laughs.

"Me, Ma." The taller one pushes his friend away.

The black lady stands still with one hand on her hip, looking mean at them. The taller sailor walks toward her in a funny way, shaking his hip from side to side and tilting his head way back. His cap falls off. He pats his imaginary beehive with his floppy wrist. The black lady does not move.

The shorter sailor drinks his beer and then drops the bottle to the ground. It smashes to a million pieces. He walks toward the black lady. "Fuck you," she says.

"Knock, knock."

"Who's there?"

"Me, Ma."

"Me Mahoo."

The sailors laugh. They laugh so hard that they both fall

to the sidewalk. The black lady turns and walks in front of our car. She holds her beehive, and her high heels click. I notice Mom intently watching the scene in front of us, and when the light turns green she doesn't beep or run the black lady over. The zipper of the black lady's dress is halfway down. The dress is lacy and blue.

With one finger, Mom lowers her dark sunglasses to the base of her nose. "That's a *mahoo*," she says and points to the black lady.

Julia's head pops up between the two front seats and stares at the lady at the end of Mom's finger. "He looks beautiful," Julia says. "But how does he grow his *chi-chi*s?"

"Kleenex," Mom answers.

After the *mahoo* walks away, after the sailors return to the bar, the car turns the corner. Julia explains to me, as Mom backs the car into a space, that *mahoo* is the Hawaiian word for a man who dresses like a woman.

After the movie, Julia and I each have soft white wontons in a clear broth for lunch at the chop suey house where Mom works. I savor the pieces of fatty *cha sui*, but drown the greens with my chopsticks. Mom eats a plate of beef *chow fun*. We eat at Wing Woo Chop Suey House because we get half off, and it's just around the corner from the theater.

Mom's waitress friend serves us. Mom tells her how good and scary the movie was. She asks Mom how she could take young kids to a movie like that.

"Mom makes us go with her," Julia pipes up.

Mom adds: "I tell them to bring their sweaters."

"Marie!" the waitress says, surprised, and laughs.

Julia and I watch an old Chinese woman holding two pink plastic shopping bags and looking through the glass door of the restaurant. The weight of the bags seems too heavy for her. She hunches over. Green leaves sprout out of the top of one of the bags. The open food market is only blocks away, near the harbor. Julia tells me that Chinatown is the oldest section of Honolulu. Ships filled with Chinese sugar cane workers arrived at the turn of the century.

A tall black lady walks beyond the glass door, and Julia points at her with her chopstick with a wonton speared on its end. Soup drips off it. "Is that one?" she asks Mom. The black lady is gone.

"Knock, knock," Julia says to me.

"Who's there?"

"Me, Ma."

"I'm not going to say it."

"But you have to," she yells. "Mom, make Michael say it. He has to say it."

SOME NIGHTS, after the chop suey house closes, Mom plays mahjongg with the other workers. As they play they watch the festive activities outside the window—the sailors, the prostitutes, the *mahoos*—as if they were a late night movie. Mom bets her evening's tips.

Mom comes home late and her noises wake me up from bad dreams. I'm dreaming about the lady vampire from the last scary movie we saw. Dad snores beside me. I want to get out of bed to see Mom but don't because she would be angry with me because it's so late. I gingerly turn over, careful not to wake Dad. Mom turns on the TV in the living room and then the water in the shower. She sneaks a peak into my room (I close my eyes tighter), and then she turns off the little table lamp I keep on because I don't like the dark. Now it is completely dark except for the light that glows eerily on the wall, coming from the TV in the living room. I tell myself to stop thinking about the vampire lady and to hurry and fall asleep. Shutting my eyes makes it worse.

A little while later I am still not asleep. I get out of bed and tiptoe to the living room. Mom sleeps on the sofa. Her long black hair is still wet. Her head lies on a white hand towel. A vibrating bright fuzz comes on the TV. When I turn it off it is completely dark. I nudge Mom and tell her to get up and go to her room. She opens her eyes and mumbles, "Go away," and pushes me away. Sometimes Mom sleeps on the sofa alone.

In the pitch dark I walk back to bed, where Dad snores. I imagine Julia alone in the other room and wonder if she is afraid. I am relieved because I get to sleep with Dad. I lay my head on a white hand towel covering the pillow and when I feel saliva slide out of my mouth and hit the towel, then I know I will soon be asleep.

ON SUNDAY evenings we usually go to the Chinese movie in Chinatown. But this night Dad stays home sick. Mom again drives around in search of a parking space, while in the front seat Julia points to every woman on the sidewalk and calls them all *mahoos*. She laughs, and I press my face against the back window. These are the stars of Chinatown. They fight with the white sailors on the sidewalks. At night old Chinese men sit on milk crates, smoke cigarettes, and watch. Mom tells Julia that if she doesn't stop pointing, they will soon come and take her away. "They don't want me," she answers. "I'm already a girl. They want Michael."

When the car stops at a light, I pull away from the window and slide over on the back seat to Mom's side of the car. Julia rolls up her window but continues to point and laugh. She tells me to look at the one in the red dress. She has long black hair and looks Oriental. She has small breasts and stands petite, more ladylike than her black friends. She is the most beautiful one, I think. But not as beautiful as Mom.

In tonight's movie the heroine is crippled and walks with crutches. Her handsome lover wears a red dress, has long black hair tied in a bun on top of his head, fights with a steel sword, and carries her through the Himalayas to a sacred pond. It is snowing. If the crippled heroine soaks her legs in the sacred pond of steaming hot water for a while, she will be cured and able to walk again. But the immediate area surrounding the pond is extremely cold. In order to enter the pond without freezing to death, one must possess a white pearl. As the crippled heroine sits on the edge of the pond with her legs immersed in the water, the pearl in hand, her lover stands alone beyond the freezing point. But suddenly he is attacked by three bad guys. He is injured and in danger. The crippled heroine shouts to him. She tosses the magic pearl to her lover. He catches it in the nick of time and flees into the freezing area. He is safe. When the bad guys follow him, they are instantly frozen. But alas, the heroine has also turned to ice, having sacrificed the pearl for her lover. He holds her frozen body and weeps.

I turn to Mom in the dark theater and see tears freeze in her eyes. I reach over and touch her hand and imagine that I am secretly passing her the soft white pearl.

ORDINARY CHINESE PEOPLE

THE WHITE man lured him out of the aisle of neatly folded Levis in the Sears boys' department, up a flight of stairs to a secluded men's room. Michael stepped up to the urinal beside the man. They did not speak. He watched the man begin to play with himself. He reached out to stroke the man's hairy arms. Michael wanted to pull the man closer to him: he wanted the man to hold him. The arms felt hard and bristly and sweaty. The man grabbed Michael's hand and guided it to his penis. It filled Michael's grip. Forcefully, the man took hold of Michael's head and pushed it downward. The man's dick smelled sour and choked him, and the man held him in place.

After he came, the man washed his hands and then walked out. The door of the men's room opened and then shut. Michael stood alone at the urinal, his half-stiffened penis in his hand.

IN HIGH SCHOOL Michael read the book *Ordinary People* and then discovered the movie version on video. He rented it and secretly watched it five times over a weekend, crying through each viewing. He fell in love with the actor Timothy Hutton and fantasized about helping his character, the melancholy teenager Conrad Jarrett. One of Michael's favorite scenes from the movie was when Conrad's mother, Beth (played by Mary Tyler Moore), asks her husband, Cal (Donald Sutherland), for the camera as Cal is about to take a picture of mother and son. She insists that she wants a picture of father and son instead. Father fidgets with the camera, unable to get the flash to work.

"Give me the camera," says Beth, her hand reaching out. "I really want to get a picture of the two of you. Give me the camera."

"Just hold on," Cal says. "I've almost got it, dear. Darn." He still can't get it to work.

"Give me the camera, Cal," Beth says again.

At this point, Conrad, all too aware of his mother's discomfort at being in a picture with him, screams, "Dad, give her the goddamn camera."

Michael wished his family were more like the Jarretts. They talked about their problems, problems that seemed real, dramatic, important.

At this time, Michael was also in love with his white track coach. After practice each evening he would linger in the locker room, dressing slowly, pretending to read a book, waiting for everyone else to leave so he could be alone with his coach. They talked about the upcoming meet, school, and the mainland. His coach was from Ohio. He had chosen to come to Hawaii after graduating from college because it was time to try being on his own. But living alone, he admitted to Michael, was difficult. The people in Hawaii were not as friendly as they were back in Ohio. Hawaii was different from the mainland. Michael told his coach that he wanted to go to the mainland for college. Quietly, Michael added that he, too, sometimes felt lonely in Hawaii. It was all part of growing up, his coach heartily reassured him. The white man's voice was like a pair of warm arms around Michael. "Don't be afraid. We all feel lonely sometimes. It's all a part of growing up, of becoming a man."

His coach was not like other men Michael knew. He was handsome, sensitive, tall — over six feet tall, the tallest man Michael had ever known. But somehow as Michael spent more time with his coach, his own loneliness grew. When he was away from the locker room, he felt depressed. He looked forward only to those intimate talks with his coach. When the coach had to leave early, he would pat Michael on the shoulder and usher him out. The clicking of the lock made Michael quiver.

Then he began to feel his coach pushing him away. The coach told Michael that everyone should be out of the locker room by seven and suggested that he go out with his teammates. Michael felt he had frightened his coach away by talking too much about his own problems. But he also knew that he had to talk privately with his coach once more, to tell him he was sorry.

Michael imagined himself as upset as Conrad Jarrett had been in the movie. And then it occurred to Michael that if he did to himself what Conrad had done to himself, then his coach would fall in love with him as he had fallen in love with Conrad.

"YOUR MOTHER is on her way," his coach said. Michael looked up at the locker-room window and imagined escaping through it. He could hide out in chaotic Waikiki; they would never find him there. But his coach would not let him out of his sight: for the first time Michael felt he had his coach's full attention. He had begged the coach not to call his mother. "This is out of my hands," the coach explained. "There are people out there who can help you."

Michael heard his mother's keys jingling outside, just as they jingled on her arrival home late at night from the restaurant. When she came home she woke up the entire apartment with her noises.

"Michael," she called. She stood at the locker room doorway. She wore a pair of blue terry cloth shorts that showed the purple veins running up her legs, the result of being on her feet all day and night at the restaurant. "Is he all right?"

"He's all right," his coach said. "Just a small cut. Not too serious. But I think you should take him to the hospital."

Michael knew that his coach was speaking too quickly for his mother to comprehend. Michael would have to explain it all again to her in Chinese. Explain what? She would ask him why he had done this to himself. He would tell her he did not feel well.

His coach was shirtless; being from the mainland, he found Hawaii too warm and often would remain shirtless throughout practice. When he had bent over to pick up Michael off the floor, Michael had become intoxicated by his coach's musky odor. His cheek had grazed his coach's hairy chest, as his coach strongly gripped his arms and pulled him up. But it was now nighttime and his mother was here, and he wished his coach would put his clothes back on. When sweat began to slide down his coach's armpits, Michael imagined himself wiping them dry with his bloody towel.

HE PULLED away from his mother, leaning against the side of the car. She stared intently, scolding him without words. It was her mah-jongg night, her only escape from the restaurant. He wondered how she had torn herself away from the game. It must have been difficult explaining to the other players that she had to leave immediately; the game needed four people to be played. Michael imagined that she had been on a winning streak when she received the phone call.

As they drove over the Ala Wai Bridge, he wanted to turn the wheel, just lean over and push it. The car would then, he hoped, knock into the curb of the sidewalk, crash into the bridge, and flip over into the canal. But were they going fast enough to accomplish such a feat? He looked at his mother. She held the wheel tight, as if expecting him to do something stupid again; she would push him away before he even had the chance to cross over to her side of the car.

In the emergency room, an old white nurse with wispy blond hair held back by gold bobby pins presented a form and a pen to Michael's mother. She held them for a few seconds before attempting to pass them to her son. He did not take them but only held the towel tighter around his wrist, in order to deflect the task of filling out the form. His mother put the paper and pen down. The nurse looked at both mother and son, astonished. After another silent moment of resistance, Michael braced his towel-wrapped wrist against the countertop and, with his left hand, picked up the pen. His mother pulled out the insurance card from her purse and slid it to him so he could copy down the policy number.

In the back, without his mother, Michael was given a compassionate look by a young Japanese lady doctor. "It'll be all right," she said plainly. Michael wondered if she had any idea why he had done this to himself. He watched her carefully stitch up the cut.

The doctor tied a knot, and Michael was reminded of how he had once accidentally unraveled his mother's knitting; he had moved the needles and yarn off the sofa to another seat so that he could sit next to his father as they watched TV. When she returned from the bathroom, after noting that she had been displaced, his mother confronted him about the unraveled knitting. Michael confessed. She hit him hard with her hand. His father surprisingly came to his defense: "He tells you he did it, and still you hit him?" She scoffed at her husband and then picked up her knitting.

His mother worked hard. She never had time to do the things she wanted to do, always having to take care of him and his father. Sometimes he thought about running away, taking some of the burden with him. Then his mother could have the time to take an ESL class at the local high school. Then she would learn how to fill out a form or write a PE note. When he felt sick (but not sick enough to skip school), he would ask her to write a note excusing him from Physical Education. He wrote out the note himself first; then she recopied it onto another sheet of paper. Her writing looked more childish than his own, and often the PE teacher would look at him suspiciously, as if questioning the note's authenticity. After she signed her name to her own handwritten note, she would look at it, without comprehension but with a small amount of pride. She had succeeded in writing English. Sometimes he would ask her to write it again, neater this time. When she refused, he grabbed it out of her hand and stuck it in his backpack.

Outside, in the hospital's waiting room, Michael's mother wrote her name over and over again on a sheet of paper, practicing for the signing of the release form.

As they drove home from the hospital, she started in. "So why did you do this?"

He did not answer her.

"Why?" Her voice drove into his head.

"I don't know."

"What don't you know? I think you think you know too much."

"I don't feel well."

"Are you sick?"

"I don't feel well." He vowed these would be his final words.

"Just like your father. Always sick. Sick in the head. Well, I'm *fan chot fay* too, sick and tired of both of you." She began to cry.

He had seen her cry only once before, not counting the many times at the movies, and that time too he had been the cause. When he was little he had run out of the apartment at the same moment that she had walked in; the screen door slammed her face. The little boy pulled back, afraid of being hit. His mother sat down at the kitchen table, her face bruised red, crying in prolonged sobs. His father sat sleeping in the living room with the TV blaring. Michael wanted his punishment, but no one gave it to him. His mother covered her face with her hand, and hugged herself with the other arm, its hand anchored at her shoulder. Had he hurt her there too? He stood there mesmerized, not knowing what to do. Eventually he retreated silently to the living room and sat beside his dozing father on the sofa. In side glances he kept watch over his mother, whimpering alone in the kitchen.

As they drove into the parking lot, Michael vowed never to make her cry again. They walked into the apartment building, and she called to him. She dried her face with her hand and then wiped the hand on her terry cloth shorts. When he felt her touch he wanted to run away.

"Michael," she said. Her hand lay heavily on his shoulder. "Don't ever do that again."

He pulled away from her and, exasperated, pleaded with her, "Stop worrying. I won't. Okay?"

Sometimes in the middle of the night, his father gets up. Michael lies in his bunk, listening: the TV clicks on, the faucet runs in the kitchen, the refrigerator door opens, the toilet flushes. He wonders if his father will ever go back to bed.

When Michael is nine he experiences his first sleepless night. He climbs down from his bunk a half dozen times to go to the bathroom. In front of the toilet, he finds that he does not really need to piss. Finally he decides to go to the living room and turns on the TV without any volume. The light of the TV illuminates the porcelain figurines displayed on the bookshelf. The Chinese gods' faces make Michael even more anxious. He lets his hand play with the sitting Buddha: his fat body mounted by five little Chinese boys; one of the boys grasps the Buddha's succulent nipple as if daring to suck it, perhaps causing the Buddha's frozen ecstatic smile. After a while his father comes into the living room. Lit by the TV, his father looks like a ghost; he squints his eyes at Michael, shakes his head, and returns to the bedroom.

His mother shouts from her bedroom. "Michael, what are you doing?"

"I can't sleep."

"Just go to bed and try to sleep. Don't think about anything."

In bed again he lies perfectly still but cannot help thinking about the day ahead: his mother works late at the restaurant. His father is always tired when he comes home from the factory. Julia doesn't talk to him anymore. He must go to school in the morning, tomorrow and forever. He begins to shake his legs back and forth. He pushes the blanket off the bed. Then he goes down to retrieve it in order to cover up his stiffened googoojai in his pajama pants, in case his mother walks into the room. He hears his father get up again. He begins to wonder what will happen if he himself does not sleep. Will he still have to go to school in the morning? It is getting dangerously late. Night and day are no longer separated by sleep; Michael can no longer go to bed, wishing away the day's problems. He wants his father to go back to his room. He forces his eyelids shut. "I can't sleep!"

When Michael woke up the next morning, his father had already left for the factory. As usual, his mother drove him to school. In the afternoon she picked him up. No more track practice, she had told him. At home she started the rice for dinner. His father cooked some fish. They ate in silence, and then his mother headed back to the restaurant for the dinner shift. Michael went to his room and climbed up to his bunk. The day darkened as he tried to sleep.

He felt someone coming up to his bed. His father climbed up the bunk and moved on all fours from the foot of the bed toward Michael. Soon his father was lying beside him. His father's arm rested on his back. It felt heavy and Michael turned his face toward the wall away from his father's fishy breath.

"Hey," his father said. He tapped his son's head with his knuckles. "Wake up."

Michael did not turn around.

"I have something to tell you."

"Leave me alone."

But his father began anyway, and kept talking. "When I was your age my family was very poor. My mother went off to work in Hong Kong. I didn't see her again until I was much older, and by that time I had forgotten what she looked like. My grandmother raised me in Macao. When I asked her for money, a few coins to buy some sweets from the vendor, she would never have anything to give me, and even scolded me for asking. One day she received an envelope, and I knew it must be from my grandfather. When I asked her if he was coming home, she told me to shut up. The letter disappeared. Several days later I asked her again for money for candy, and instead of giving me her usual refusal, she grumbled and told me that I was always wasting money, all the while going to the drawer to fetch a coin. She carried it over to me, and with a final complaint threw it on the ground. It rolled past me out the front door, and into the gutter. All afternoon I kept reaching down that dark hole trying to fish out that coin." Michael's father suddenly released his son, climbed down from the bed, and walked out of the room.

ONE WEEKEND, a month later, his father took him to a local dim sum restaurant. After pouring tea and picking out a few baskets of hot steaming dumplings, his father started, "Michael, you've got to start thinking about the future. You've got to start planning for the future."

Michael was not expected to respond. A wave of a hand as if shooing away a fly, or a frowning, questioning glare was enough to encourage his father to continue speaking. His father's words were like firecrackers snapping off an endless burning vine, and all Michael could do was wait until the flames died. He knew better than to agree with his father—then his father would have nothing else to say, and they would be forced to sit in uncomfortable silence together for the remainder of the meal.

"You've got to start thinking about college, maybe study to be a lawyer, or even better, a doctor. You'll go to the University of Hawaii. You've got to get a good job, because it's your responsibility as the number-one and only son to take care of your parents when we get old."

Michael closed his eyes at this point to make his father disappear. "I'm going to college," he started, "but not here in Hawaii. To a mainland school." *Far away from here.*

"If I had the money I would not hesitate one minute to send you to a mainland college. I've heard the schools there are much better than Hawaiian schools. If I had the money I would. But money is tight when you have a family. When you marry and have your own family, you will know how frustrating it is when you want to give your children things but can't because you don't have the money to buy them. Without money you can't go out, you can't buy a house, you can't even eat."

Michael shoveled another fatty dumpling into his mouth.

"Don't be like me. Don't get yourself stuck in a job for twenty years, going nowhere, making the same money. And look at your mother. That woman can never hold on to any money she makes. Spend, spend, spend. There's no tomorrow with her."

When his parents watched their Chinese soaps at night on the VCR after his mother came home from work, his father would inevitably fall asleep. His mother would pause the VCR and tell his father to go to bed. He would get up from the recliner and ask her to turn it off and come to bed with him. She unpaused the VCR. He stood at the doorway suspended between the darkness behind him and the bright TV screen in front. His eyes were closing. The volume of the TV was loud. Romantic music played in the background of the Chinese soaps. Wei asked Marie once more to come with him. When she didn't answer or move, he turned into the dark bedroom alone.

Michael wondered why his parents, with their differences, got married in the first place. Was it because of love, companionship, need? Sometimes he imagined his mother marrying a rich white man. They would be living in Kahala, the most expensive neighborhood in Honolulu. But if that had been the case, would he have been born? No. He was the unique and abnormal product of his Chinese parents.

"Later is too late. Don't be like me," his father repeated. "It's too late for me. The reason I came to Hawaii, the reason I left China in the first place, was for you. So my family could have a better life."

Michael felt the rebellion in his heart weaken. He did not want to disappoint his father any more than his father had already disappointed himself. Like his father, he would fail. This bonded them: they were number-one sons in appearance only.

IN THE middle of the night, in bed, Michael listened to his father get up and go to the living room. In his mind, he saw his father sitting in the dark on the sofa, silently facing the maniacally smiling Buddha, and Michael wondered: When did his father give up the hope of ever fishing out the coin from the gutter?

III

CULTURAL REVOLUTION

MICHAEL FELT too nauseated to look for the muffled laughter on the bus, more like an American school bus than a Greyhound. It rode slowly without shock absorbers to Yuan from Macao, sixty miles over the Communist border. He felt his father sitting too close to him and inched toward the window. Outside was a monotonous field of short rice plants, jutting out of a mirror of water. Occasionally there stood a half-naked Chinese farmer under an oversized straw hat.

"American school has taught him to forget all of his Chinese," Michael's father had said repeatedly to relatives in Hong Kong, with both shame and pride in his voice. When they had arrived there two weeks before, Michael had found his relatives' accents difficult to understand; still, he had always understood his father, even though sometimes he pretended not to. And by the end of the first week he had found himself deciphering his relatives' conversations, though he still could not readily contribute to them.

Father and son had spent eight days in Hong Kong with uncles, aunts, and countless cousins. Every meal took place at a round table with a lazy susan, spinning around Chinese delicacies: dim sum, roast suckling pig, shark fin soup, sautéed frog legs. In large restaurants, noisy family parties were partitioned off in sections, each complete with a color TV and a mah-jongg set. The city's noise and mugginess, so unlike Hawaii's drier heat, made Michael ill. A doctor gave him a prescription for antibiotics and instructions to drink bottled water to clean out his system. Then they took a ferry to Macao. There they stayed with an aunt in a cramped second-floor apartment (his great-grandmother Mai Wah's old apartment).

On the bus to his father's home village, Michael complained about stomach cramps. His father answered, "If it's not one thing, it's another. It was a waste of money to bring you here in the first place." August was the only time that this trip to the homeland had been possible. Michael was going off to college in two weeks, to the U.S. mainland. He could hardly wait. Five thousand miles separated Hawaii from Chicago, white-man's land. In the bus, Michael again turned to the window, only to discover there a reflection of a white man's face staring at his reflection and laughing.

This was the real China. In high school Michael had learned about Sun Yat Sen, the Japanese invasion, and the Cultural Revolution. He had pieced these facts together with the few stories that he had heard from his father when he was little.

Michael had found these stories unsatisfying and had written in his mind his own version of his father's life in China. When his father was just a baby, the Japanese had invaded his village. Michael remembered the story of his father's grandmother fleeing, fearless, with his infant father in her arms to hide in the rice fields. But on this trip he cared little about the real bits of his father's past that they discovered. It was already too late; he wanted to be on his way to Chicago, writing his own future.

As his father led the way out of the bus, Michael turned around to look at the man in the front seat. He looked like an American college student, with short blond hair, white skin, a thick, strong neck like a football player's, a few strands of chest hair pushing up from his polo shirt's open collar. His hand searched his backpack, pulling a camera out of the pouch. He looked up as Michael passed.

The hotel was an ugly square building, six stories high, the tallest around. The lobby was decorated in fifties style, a green-and-white tile floor speckled with black dots, a simulated wood counter, the reception desk with a matching freestanding backboard. Off to one side, a pair of glass doors led to a restaurant with tables covered by stained red cloth. Chinese men and women, uncomfortably dressed in black polyester trousers and wrinkled white shirts buttoned to their necks, lazily carried trays of water glasses and bland Chinese dishes.

After signing for their hotel room, Michael's father insisted that they deposit their bags behind the counter and begin an immediate search for the old home. "I don't know if it's still there. It's out by the rice fields. I can't believe it will look the same after all these years." Michael hated seeing his father so excited. The white man from the bus walked into the lobby, his backpack zipped, the camera heavy in his hands. He walked past

Michael to the front desk. "We shouldn't just leave the bags behind the counter," Michael said. "They won't be safe."

He watched his father examining the receptionist behind the counter. She signed the white man into the guest book. Thick, black-framed glasses accentuated the roundness of the young woman's face. The line of her bangs was uneven, and a strand of black hair strayed noticeably behind the lens of her glasses. She smiled with crooked buck teeth. The white man showed her his American passport. "You go ahead, Dad," Michael said. "I want to go upstairs with the bags and lie down for just a little while. I'll catch up with you later. It must've been something I ate at dim sum this morning."

He and the white man rode the elevator up together to the same floor. Michael commented on how horrible the bus ride had been. They looked at each other once more before going to their separate rooms.

Michael loved air-conditioning. He lay down on one of the two twin beds. He was glad that he and his father would be sleeping separately tonight. He rolled from side to side and then jumped up, giving it the appearance of being slept in. He then left the room and proceeded down the hallway to the white man's room; the door was open a crack. He stepped in and closed it behind him.

"Quiet. We'd better not talk," the white man said. "Thin walls. My name's Alex." He moved closer. He was twice Michael's breadth, but the top of his head came up only to Michael's eyes. Michael was skinny, like a typical Cantonese man—like his father. But he had grown tall like his mother. "All that milk and white bread has made him so tall," his father had explained to the Hong Kong relatives.

His feet hit the footboard of the bed. "Damn," he called out. "This bed is too short."

"We should try to be a little quieter. We *are* in China."

Michael liked the feel of Alex's thick flesh and hairy chest. They held each other and kissed, slowly turning their bodies sideways. Alex ran his hand down Michael's knobby spine to his fleshy buttocks and slowly patted him there, lulling him. Michael remembered sleeping in the same bed with his father when he was little; his father would pat him on the butt until he fell asleep.

After sex, Alex dozed off beside him. Michael avoided touching Alex by leaning to the other side of the bed, almost falling off. He did not want to sleep here, but neither did he want to get up to look for his father. This trip to the homeland had already gone on too long. His feet knocked against the baseboard again. "This is ridiculous."

Alex opened his eyes. "What?"

"The footboard. I can't sleep here."

Alex sat up and massaged Michael's feet. "Is that better, baby?" Alex climbed on top of Michael, pinning him down at the shoulders. "You're so beautiful," he said to Michael. Michael closed his eyes as Alex kissed him on his pressed lips and then on his neck, where he sucked wet and long.

"You're going to get me into trouble," Michael said. "Let me go." He jumped out of bed and stood in front of the mirror on the wall. A red spot had appeared on his neck.

"If I spoke Chinese to you, would you be able to understand me?" Alex asked.

"If you do, I'll ignore you like I do my father." He didn't like Alex being so familiar with him. They had met only an hour ago. Michael did not even find him attractive. He had only looked at Alex on the bus because he was the first white man he had seen in a while.

MICHAEL DID not say no when Alex asked to come along to look for his father and the old home. Alex would serve as a welcome buffer between him and his father. Outside the hotel Alex immediately began to photograph everything, like a Japanese tourist. "Everything is so simple," he said. "It's like the nineteen-fifties. A village, a country where time stood still. I bet this place is exactly the way your father remembers it." Michael stood by silently as Alex bargained with an old ricksha driver. He was jealous of Alex's perfect accent and diction. Alex asked the old man how far away the rice fields were. The old man's legs were dark and wrinkled like beef jerky; lines divided his face. He laughed, showing a single tooth, as Alex took his picture, and then he mounted the rusty bicycle.

"This white man knows how to speak Chinese," the old man shouted to another driver. The black hood overhead focused their view to the back of the driver and the road ahead. The old man stood on the pedals, pushed downward, and started the bike in motion.

"I'm surprised that he's able to drive this thing," Michael said.

"I was in Beijing in the spring," Alex told him. "It's a wonderful place. Even more exciting than here. Canton and the South have been influenced and spoiled by Hong Kong."

Alex told Michael that he was studying in Hong Kong, where gay life was much more in the open. He made occasional trips to the mainland. But Michael didn't want to hear about

Alex's Chinese experiences and instead told Alex about his going to college in Chicago the following month. "The Midwest is white mall country. It's culturally dead," Alex remarked. "I don't know what you're going to do there." Michael scowled at Alex.

People scurried out of the ricksha's way. A thin sheet of dust hovered above the dirt road. Shops—groceries, bakeries, drug stores—occupied the first floor of the buildings. Above, families were crowded into two-room apartments; children hung out of windows while their laundry blew lifelessly on the line, bleached shirts and trousers. The ricksha drove between the buildings, down an alleyway. Wooden stands sold local produce and delicacies: wilted greens, hanging roasted ducks and dogs, and frogs in straw baskets, climbing on top of each other. An old woman sat on a stool, twisting a live chicken's neck.

"Did you meet anyone in Beijing?" Michael asked.

"Any gay men? Yes."

"That's amazing. Chinese gay men. Chinese men gay in Beijing."

"And what about yourself?"

"I've been corrupted by America," Michael said. "You are the *bok gwei*, the white devil. First the man you corrupted in Beijing, and now me."

"I don't think I could've added to your corruption."

"There weren't any gay men in China before the white man came along," Michael joked. "Except perhaps the drag-queen opera singers. But every culture has its transvestites."

Alex asked, "How about you? Did you meet anyone in Hong Kong?"

"Are you serious? I've been with my father for the entire two weeks. We even had to sleep in the same bed at my aunt's in Macao. Her apartment originally belonged to my great-grandmother. One of the bathrooms is a dark room with a hole in the floor."

The ricksha drove out of the village, along the rice fields, into the quieter countryside. Ahead was a small group of houses. Michael knocked Alex's hand off his knee. "Stop it. We're almost there," he said. He began to wonder whether bringing Alex along was such a good idea. What if Alex told his father what had happened in the hotel room? But his father was probably too naive to understand, even if told. And why would Alex tell his father? Michael had considered that he was doing the white tourist a favor by bringing him along to visit a real Chinese home. "So tell me about the man you met in Beijing."

Alex again placed his hand on Michael's knee. "We met under the big Mao picture in Tiananmen Square, near the entrance to the Forbidden City. That's where you hang out if you want to pick up a local man. They're especially interested in white men. But they're very careful, of course. It's a serious crime in China."

"Who did you meet?"

"Ming Tim. He was a little older than me. Very severe. Dark-skinned and lanky. I saw him. He saw me. We looked at each other for about fifteen minutes, and then as I walked away, he followed. Cruising's the same in every country. After I caught up to him, we continued walking side by side without speaking. Then he told me that he had to leave. He had to pick up his wife at the factory! In China it's difficult to get your own apartment if you're not married. The only alternative is to live with your parents for the rest of your life. As he walked away, he said, 'I want to see you again. Tomorrow. I'll meet you in front of your hotel.' Then he ran off, around a corner."

"Did you spend your entire time in Beijing under the Mao picture?" Michael asked.

"No. Do you want to hear the rest of this story or not, smartass?"

"Yes, but hold off. Here's the old home. Now, no gay stuff, or I'll drown you in the rice fields."

"Oh, that could be fun."

"Stop it."

The ricksha slowed and then stopped. On one side of the road stood a row of five attached brick houses, all alike. On the other side were the rice fields, parallel rows of weedlike plants, rows and rows nestled in soft, dark mud and extending to the mountains, shrouded by clouds, beyond. A farmer stood in ankle-high water, his face hidden by his straw hat. He held up a plant to the sun. His skin, dark like leather, stretched over his protruding ribs.

"He's beautiful," Alex said.

"Rice queen."

"I like the Chinese culture and its men."

Out of the center house, Michael's father emerged, looking a little out of place in his polo shirt and belted trousers. "Nothing has changed," he said and shook his head.

Michael and Alex walked toward him. "I used to live here," he said. "Even a few of the old neighbors are still here."

Alex stepped up to Michael's father. Michael froze. "Hello, I'm Alex. I'm staying at your hotel, where I met your son." Alex shook Mr. Lau's hand. "He told me that he was going to look for his father's old home. What a wonderful idea! I had to invite myself along. I'm a student at the University of Hong Kong. Modern Chinese history. Michael told me all about your visit back to the homeland. It's great that you can come back after all these years."

"Hello." Michael's father gave the stranger a lipless smile, and then walked directly over to his son. "Are you still sick? It took you a long time to get here. I was already planning to go back to the hotel. It's too hot. Is the hotel room air-conditioned? I'm feeling a little sick myself."

Michael was relieved by his father's cool reception of Alex, though he was disappointed that the only white man in this tiny Chinese village did not pique his father's curiosity.

"They have only an outhouse in back," his father continued. "The same one that was here when I used to live here."

From behind his father, two old women emerged from the green doorway. Sticks, stones, weeds, and bricks littered the front yard.

"He isn't your son, is he?" said the younger of the two old women, pointing to the white man. Her hair was silver and thinning, and she smiled silver teeth. Beside her was an even older woman, hunched over like an insect. She looked only at the garbage on the ground. She was blind. Underneath surviving white strands of hair, her hard scalp was dotted with dark liver spots.

"No, *this* is my son. Michael, show your respect to Wu Tai Tai and her daughter, Sui Lee."

Michael held Sui Lee's hand. He could feel only bones. Her thin smile grew, and her eyes strained to open wider. He was afraid to shake the blind mother's hand.

"They lived next door when I lived here. Now they live in my grandmother's house. The house is exactly the way that I remembered it."

Alex held his camera to the group. "I want a picture of this moment." The camera clicked. Michael turned and stared at him with contempt: he began to despise Alex's enthusiasm for his family.

"Your son is tall," the old daughter said. She held her hand above her eyes to block the sun as she looked Michael up and down.

INSIDE, THE old blind mother poured glasses of hot tea from an aluminum thermos and passed them to her daughter to hand to the men, who sat in large, uncomfortable wooden chairs decorated with carvings of flowers on the arms and a Chinese character on the back. The door stood open, letting in a warm breeze and a view of the constant rice fields.

"Do you know what this means?" Alex whispered to Michael, pointing to the character on the chair.

Michael did not respond.

"Peaceful."

Michael turned away. The old women spoke with heavy local accents. He strained his eyes to follow their conversation. His head began to ache.

"They're talking about you," Alex said. "Your father says you're going to college in Chicago. The old daughter said, 'Such a foreign, faraway-sounding place.' "

Michael hated Alex for interpreting his father's conversation, for explaining the writing on the chair, for hiring the ricksha. Except for being white, Alex was the perfect Chinese son: and Michael wasn't. He found Alex's preference for Chinese men odd because he himself had never been attracted to them. They would seem too much like his father: bony and devoid of chest hair. He looked out at the farmer. He wanted to hear the rest of Alex's pickup story. It seemed slightly perverse. If he could only get Alex alone again for a little while, he could hear the rest of the story and then tell him to go away.

"Not much has changed since you left," said Sui Lee, the old daughter. "The old school is still there. If I remember correctly, you were such a bad boy, Mr. Lau. Crying all the way to school every day. A new house went up further down the road, maybe ten years ago. America must be so exciting compared to all of this. All the furniture is still here. You didn't come back for anything? Did you?" Her eyes widened. "We haven't thrown anything out. It's all still here. We weren't sure whether or not you were coming back. Why would you want to? America sounds like a dream come true."

Hawaii is not America, Michael thought. Chicago, the mainland, is America. He looked out the door at the rice fields again. The Japanese had invaded this village a long time ago, before the faded Mao picture on the wall, before the color TV, before Peking became Beijing. Slowly and patiently, the farmer tended his crop. The plants came up to his knees. His great-grandmother had been a brave woman. But for a moment it didn't seem possible that even an old Chinese woman could safely hide her small body among those short plants, in all that water.

Michael grew tired of listening to Chinese. "Let's look around," he said to Alex, and led the way past the old mother.

"What a big boy," she said, her sightless eyes still turned to the ground.

THE ADJACENT room was two stories high but still dark. There were no windows, just an open doorway in the far corner letting in some light. Against the left wall a wooden staircase led to a small platform and a closed door. On the right was a bed neatly made up with white sheets and an embroidered red quilt. A sewing machine sat in the center of the room. Yards of olive green cloth unraveled from the tabletop onto the floor.

"I bet the real bedroom's upstairs," Alex surmised.

"Finish your story," Michael said. "I want to know what happened. Every juicy little detail."

"You want me to tell you now? Here?"

"Yeah, while they're in the other room." Michael sat down on the bed.

"All right. Where was I? The next day Ming Tim was waiting for me outside my hotel. 'I've got it all figured out,' he said. 'My wife's spending the night at her mother's tonight. Forty miles away from here. I'll take her to the bus station and make sure she gets on the right bus. I'll meet you here again tonight, at nine o'clock.' I agreed, and then he hurried away again."

"This bed is hard as a rock." Michael moved his hand across the floral embroidery of the quilt. "Sorry for interrupting. Go on."

"You sure you don't want to listen to them out there instead? I'll translate for you. You can hear my story later tonight — in my room. Your father and those two old women are talking about the real China. I want to know why the old mother is blind. She wasn't born that way, you know. The part of her face around her eyes seemed pushed in. But I can't really tell. She won't look up. I guess she doesn't have a reason to. They say that if you weren't born blind but became blind, you would remember the last thing you saw."

"I don't care about her. Just tell me the rest of your story." Michael enjoyed depriving Alex of a real Chinese story.

"That night I met Ming Tim outside my hotel. His cap was pulled low to his face. He led me to a darkened alleyway and handed me a Mao jacket. I wore it over my own jacket. He pushed another cap on my head. The way I was dressed, I almost looked Chinese.

"At the mouth of the courtyard of an apartment complex, Ming Tim pulled me aside again. 'Look at the ground,' he said. 'Don't look up until you are inside my apartment. We'll walk to the entrance now. There may be people around. When you see a light, put your sleeve over your mouth. Stoop over a little. If anyone sees you, they'll think that you're a sick relative of my wife. Keep your eyes down. Don't look up.

" 'If you can't walk straight, watch my feet. Don't walk too close to me. And don't ever touch me. At least not until we are inside.' He laughed for the first time.

"First I saw the dirt courtyard floor for about a hundred yards, then I almost tripped up a short flight of stairs at the entrance to the building. The lobby's tiled floor was lime-green. I kept looking for Ming's feet. We stopped at the beginning of a flight of stairs.

" 'Keep one hand on the wall, the other over your mouth,' he said. 'Let's go.' My Chinese was not as good back then. I was afraid that I had misunderstood him. I was sweating under all those clothes. He pushed me against the wall. 'Someone is coming.' "

At that moment, Michael's father entered the room, Sui Lee following behind.

Michael stood up from the bed. "What's upstairs, Dad?"

His father looked at him and then at the wrinkled quilt on the bed. "Don't lie on someone else's bed," he said in English. "You're not still sick, are you?"

"No. What's upstairs?"

Alex took a picture of the sewing machine. The flash shocked the room to momentary life. The old daughter jumped back.

"Why are you taking a picture of this junk?" Michael asked Alex.

"Upstairs was my grandmother's old bedroom, your great-grandmother's room," Michael's father said.

"We don't ever go up there," Sui Lee said excitedly. "We sleep down here." She pointed to the bed.

Michael's father walked up the creaking stairs, followed by Michael and then Alex.

Michael turned to Alex and said, "Take another picture and I'll break your camera."

Halfway up, his father turned to Michael and said, "I may have to use that outhouse after all. I don't think that I can wait until we get back to the hotel."

Michael rolled his eyes at his father.

His father looked down at his neck. "What's that?"

Michael knew that he was referring to the hickey. He pulled up his shirt collar. "It's nothing. I think it's a rash."

"I hope you don't have to see another doctor. If it's not one thing, it's another."

As they continued up the stairs, Michael wondered if Alex was planning to join them for dinner, further intruding on him and his father. But if he didn't have dinner with them, Michael imagined, Alex might wander around the marketplace and pick up a local farmer at a noodle stand. Another exciting Chinese experience for the white man.

Meanwhile Michael and his father would probably have another bland Chinese meal in a hotel restaurant, neither one having anything to say to the other. The food off the streets of China was too dangerous for their weak stomachs. In Macao, he and his father had bowls of steamed mussels from a street vendor. Michael had vomited all night into a plastic bucket beside the bed. His father climbed over him out of bed and woke up the old aunt sleeping on the rattan sofa in the living room. Querulously, he asked her to brew some roots. When she entered the bedroom, Michael saw that her blouse was half-unbuttoned; she had pulled it on before coming in. He could see the shadows of her neck tendons as she set the bowl down beside the bed and picked up the bucket. She poured it out in the squat toilet, rinsed it in the kitchen sink, and brought it back to him.

"You're spoiling this entire trip," his father muttered from his side of the bed.

"Leave me alone." Michael held his breath and drank the bitter tea in one tasteless swallow.

"Here, put this on your chest," his father said to him.

"What is it?"

"Tiger balm."

"No." Michael felt his father's hand spreading the greasy, sweet, stinging ointment on his chest.

"You're so skinny."

"Just like you."

ON THE stairway, Michael looked past Alex at the old daughter, standing frozen below. She looked up at the three of them, each one appearing less Chinese from top to bottom. The wood of the stairs squeaked painfully with the weight of human bodies for the first time in so many years. Sui Lee clutched the railing; her foot mounted the first step and then stopped.

In the bedroom, a large bed draped with canopies of cobwebs and dusty, motheaten sheets sprawled in the center. The mattress was eaten with rat holes. The engravings of the headboard told a tale of court life in ancient China. Facing the foot of the bed was a matching bureau, and on the wall above it a white rectangle, lighter than the rest of the wall, where something used to hang, perhaps a mirror. Closed wooden shutters trapped a musty odor. They would open onto a view of the rice fields. Carved on the wood were more characters and floral scenes.

"I slept here with my grandmother after my grandfather went off to work in the coal mines in South America," Michael's father said.

Michael remembered his father telling him that his grandfather had died in the mines there.

"Why haven't the old women come up here?" Alex asked.

"This house still belongs to my grandmother," Mr. Lau stated. "This is her room. Those two old women only live here."

At the bedroom doorway, Michael watched the perfect son-and-father team read the writing on the shutters together. Below, at the foot of the staircase, the old daughter was joined by her mother. They looked upward together. Maybe they were afraid that they would have to leave the house. His father would discover things missing, accuse them of theft. Michael surmised that the old daughter had sold the mirror that had originally hung on the wall above the bureau in order to buy the sewing machine, so that she would not need to leave her mother home alone all day. Her crime justified. His father stood close to Alex, their fingers touching the shutters.

"I can't read this," Alex said. "It's faded away too much." He tried to pull them open.

Michael's father hit away Alex's hand. "Don't. They've never been opened. My grandmother never opened them."

IN THE kitchen the old daughter explained to Alex how the gas canister was hooked up to the stone stove. "We refill it only once a month," she said. "I don't do much cooking. Two old women don't eat much." The old mother poured more glasses of hot tea. Michael sat on a stool, held up Alex's camera, and looked through the viewfinder out the back door. His father ventured timidly to the outhouse with a few sheets of tissue in his hand. The chickens in the yard scurried out of the way. Once his father was safe inside, under the thatched roof of the small stone closet, Michael snapped the picture.

"Come away from that wok," Michael called to Alex, "and tell me the end of your story. What happens once you get inside Mao's apartment?"

"Ming's. Now? In front of these two innocent old women?" Alex asked.

"They won't understand. Let these two old relics hear. Nothing else exciting happens here. Imagine living your entire life in this house, in this village. Tell me the end of your story before my father gets back from his reunion with the outhouse."

Alex took a glass of hot tea from the old mother's offering hands and pulled up a stool next to Michael. With wide eyes the old daughter stood over them, listening to the foreign words. "Once we were in the apartment, Ming double-locked the door. Then I heard another man's laughter. 'It's okay,' Ming said. Another Chinese man was sitting in front of the TV. He was younger, my age. I don't remember his name. I took off the Mao jacket and cap, and Ming and his friend took everything else off for me. They were so excited. They ran their hands through my chest and pubic hair, gently pulling at it with their fingers. Next they cupped their hands all over me, as if measuring my body, amazed by its size.

"Then we took a shower together. It wasn't a regular shower, like what you're used to in America. It was a small room, a single window up high like in a jail cell, and a drain in the center of the white tile floor. They sat on a bench across from me, re-marking, and their fingers pointing at me, as I poured buckets of warm water over myself. We talked about America and China. They told me that they wanted to visit America. That nearly killed me, sitting there naked, listening to them tell me that. We can visit them and see how they live, but they can't do the same. And to think how dangerous it was to have me there.

"Later on, we went back to the room and fucked."

"How?"

"I'll show you later back in my hotel room," Alex teased, taking sips of his warm tea. "Let me finish my story." He went on. "Sometime before dawn, Ming pushed me out of bed and told me to get dressed. When I reached for the Mao jacket, Ming held onto it. 'It's late,' he said. 'No one will see you leav-ing.' So on the way out, I saw what I couldn't see when I came in: the stairs, the cracks on the wall, the single light bulb hanging in the entranceway. Outside we walked together for maybe a hundred yards beyond the complex before he said, 'You go back alone now.' I reached out to hug him, but he had already begun to walk away. There was no moon out that night. I strained my eyes to look for him. I felt so lonely walking back to my hotel room alone."

"That's it?" Michael said, disappointed. "Nobody gets caught? No one gets in trouble?"

Michael's father stepped over the threshold into the kitchen. "Let's go back to the hotel. The outhouse is disgusting. The smell . . . there are flies and bugs all over the place. Lucky that old woman's blind."

IN THE front yard of the old home, they shook hands with the two old women, and Michael's father handed them each several Hong Kong dollars. They humbly thanked him, shaking their heads from side to side, proclaiming, "No, no. This is too much. You are too generous." Michael stepped away from his father, followed by Alex. Through the viewfinder of the camera, Michael looked at the rice fields. Still only one lonely farmer. He looked up from beneath his hat but was still too far away for Michael to see his face, to discover his age. He could have been eighteen or as old as his father.

"Go out there and pick up that farmer," Michael ordered Alex. "You *bok gwei*, bringing your evil ways to China, ruining simple people's lives."

"What are you talking about? Homosexuality exists in every culture. It's not exclusively white."

"But you think you're our savior. The great white hope, aren't you?" Michael retorted. "We Chinese all want white men, no? Because we want to be like you . . ."

"Here, give me the camera and let me get a picture of you and your father in front of the ancestral Chinese home."

"I don't want to be like you."

"I told you my story, now give me back my camera and get in the picture, Emperor." Alex grabbed hold of Michael's arm.

"No." Michael pulled away from Alex and the camera fell

onto the ground. The back flipped open, exposing all the film to daylight.

"I don't believe you," Alex said. "You're a real fuckin' baby."

"Go away, *bok gwei*," Michael said. "It's been fun. I'll be seeing you around."

Alex stared at Michael, shocked. For a moment Michael feared that he would say something to his father and the two old women. But would they even understand? The three of them stood, smiling and nodding. His father fidgeted back and forth. He still had not gone to the bathroom.

Alex bent down to retrieve his camera. "What's your fuckin' problem?" he said to Michael.

"Go away."

Alex began to walk alongside the field alone, the lonely tourist. As he walked, he kept watch over the farmer in the field. Michael imagined Alex having sex with the farmer and then saw himself with the farmer. The farmer's body would be skinny like his own. With each movement, their elbows, knees, bones would knock painfully together.

His father continued to pace. Hurry, hurry, Michael thought. Did his father suspect how differently his son had turned out from what he had wanted? His father had told his mother, "If I don't take him to China now, he'll forget that he was ever Chinese once he gets to Chicago." His father should never have left China: would he have turned out straight then? *I am different from you, Dad. I'm not Chinese. This is your homeland. Not mine.*

"I'll always remember these rice fields," his father said to the old women. "It's so peaceful here. What a green land of comfort. I remember the story my grandmother told me about how the rice fields saved our lives. How she ran out there when the Japanese came marching through. How she lay low in the mud with me wrapped in her arms."

The old blind mother looked up from the ground. Her eyes ached to open. "Is that the fairy tale Mai Wah told you?" she asked. Her voice rose in the heat.

"No, Mother," the old daughter gasped. "Please."

"You were in town that day, Sui Lee, when they came through. You did not see firsthand the horror the Japanese brought with them. You did not see what happened to these people here. I was standing in this field with your grandfather that day, Mr. Lau."

"My grandfather was in South America at the time," he replied agitated. "You must be mistaken. It was a long time ago."

"I'll never forget," she continued. "Your grandfather couldn't see that Japanese soldier approaching him from behind. When the soldier called to him it was already too late. Your grandfather started to run. You can't run in this mud even if your life depended on it. And besides, where was he running to? The mountains, so far away? The soldier took aim. I jumped on that Jap's back, and together the soldier and I fell to the ground. He pushed me off, got up, and shot your grandfather down."

"Enough!" the old daughter cried.

"My grandfather was not here when the Japanese came. He died in the South American coal mines."

"Your grandmother was probably too angry and upset to bother to tell a little boy the truth." The old mother continued. "From the fields I could see all of these brick houses. The killings, the rapes, the looting. But I could not hear a sound, not a single cry for help. It's so quiet out there. You can see these houses from miles away.

"I saw Mai Wah looking down at us from her bedroom window, her face framed by the open shutters. She had witnessed the execution of her own husband. I was told that it was then that she ran off with you in her arms and hid in the outhouse. She stayed in that darkened, stinking closet until we found her there two days later. That outhouse saved your life."

"No," Michael's father muttered. "That's not true." He stood frozen.

"Believe me, Mr. Lau," the old mother pleaded. "It's time you knew the truth. Your grandfather was murdered." She brought her hand to her face, her wristbone knocking her forehead to protect her blind eyes from the sun. "It was the last thing I saw before the soldier stabbed my eyes with his rifle."

Michael reached out to steady his shaking father. He patted him on the back. His father, shaking his head, began to walk away. He looked as if he wanted to vomit.

Michael looked back at the mother and daughter carefully framed by the green mouth of the door. Their bony fists grasped the dollars as if they were ancient prostitutes. Bricks and planks littered the ground. Slowly, his father's old home crumbled away.

THAT EVENING they ate an early dinner in the hotel restaurant. "She's a crazy old woman. She doesn't know what she's talking about," his father said and then was silent for the remainder of the meal. What did it matter after all these years? Michael thought.

Lying in bed, Michael could not sleep; his feet knocked

against the footboard. He turned to see the quiet face of his sleeping father. The air-conditioner hummed. His father remembered the past one way. He would not believe any other story. His father would never fathom the story of his son's homosexual future.

The next morning they passed up the dim sum breakfast downstairs for packaged biscuits and boiled water. It was still early when they boarded the bus. They were heading back to Hong Kong for a couple of days; from there they would fly back to Hawaii. Michael would leave for Chicago soon after. His father dozed off beside him, their arms touching as the bus rocked on the bumpy dirt road.

Michael looked at his own reflection in the window and then outside at the rice fields. Beyond the fields, the sun was coming up over the peaks of the faraway mountains. Slowly the sunlight erased his reflection from the glass. The farmer in the field took off his straw hat. His face was gaunt, tired, resigned: an old man's face. The voices and the laughter on the bus melded into a single, violent hum. The farmer, upright and unmoving, began to sink. Michael ran toward him. His sneakers moved sluggishly in the mud. The glassy water took hold of the farmer's trousered legs, embraced his naked stomach and chest —the same color as the mud—and swallowed the bulging veins of his neck. The Chinese man's eyes turned back into his head. Michael fell onto the rice field expanding out forever around him.

A NOTE ABOUT THE AUTHOR

Norman Wong was born and raised in Honolulu, Hawaii. In 1986 he took his BA in English Literature from the University of Chicago, and in 1990 he received his MA from the Writing Seminars of the Johns Hopkins University. His stories have appeared in *The Kenyon Review, Men on Men 4: Best New Gay Fiction, The Asian/Pacific American Journal of Literature, The Threepenny Review, The Little Magazine,* and *Bakunin.* He lives in New York City.